# THE THINGS I DIDN'T DO

## CHARLOTTE BARNES

Print ISBN 978-1-914614-70-5

# ALSO BY CHARLOTTE BARNES

<u>SUSPENSE THRILLERS:</u>

Intention

All I See Is You

Sincerely, Yours

---

<u>CRIME:</u>

**The DI Melanie Watton Series**

The Copycat (book one)

The Watcher (book two)

The Cutter (book three)

# I

# ERICA

## CHAPTER ONE

I didn't give the agency my real name.

On the morning she was due to arrive, I got up earlier than usual. The world was just about yawning awake by the time I was ready for my second cup of tea. I'd saved my cigarette for this. I waited for the kettle to whistle; lined up teabag with spoon with Mayfair Superking. I only allowed myself one cigarette a day; I was going to get my money's worth. While the water boiled, I studied the black packaging of the cigarette box, still sitting on the windowsill. It would tempt me throughout the day. There was a small foetus and a tagline on the dangers of smoking. I'd had this warning more than any of the others and I always wondered whether the assistants serving me my vice picked the label deliberately; as though my wisps of grey weren't signal enough that child-bearing years were behind me. Even if they weren't, though, the threat of infertility didn't bother me – that's what the other flavours of warnings were for. Still, I turned the foetus away and then I checked the time – again. It was, I estimated, the length of a cup of tea before she was due.

The email that had been forwarded over was signed *Prue*. But at the bottom of the non-disclosure agreement she'd signed

Prudence: Prudence S. Carr. In the days since, I'd been wondering what the S might stand for, whether I might be able to tell when I saw her in person. I'd googled her, of course, at the advice of my solicitor. Though I hadn't made specific requests when we'd approached the agency, only that they supplied a woman, Colin had suggested I check her over digitally before committing. Prue had a safe and sound internet presence though; one that said, quite loudly, *I don't share my personal life here.* Although she had shared awards, collaborative projects, qualifications, client testimonials. She was a walking advertisement for herself.

'She looks to take herself seriously,' I'd said to Colin, my mobile pressed between ear and shoulder so I could continue to scroll, make notes, scroll, make notes...

'We'll see how serious she is when we suggest two NDAs.'

I didn't like his tone.

'Are you expecting her to have a problem with it?'

He hesitated. 'I think... I think we need to be prepared for her to be nervous.'

'About the project?'

'Yes, Erica, about the project.'

He spoke to me how my husband might have done if he were irritated with me over something. I'd put up with it then – that's marriage – but I wouldn't put up with it from someone who I was paying hard-inherited money to speak to. 'The NDA protects me, doesn't it, whether she's nervous or not.'

'Yes,' he'd answered plainly, as though he thought I was being sincere. 'But, Erica–'

'But nothing. Send the drafts over to the agency. If she signs, she signs. If she doesn't then I'm sure they or somewhere else will have someone on their books who's less... nervy.'

The kettle blew time. I splashed water in the mug and added equal parts milk and sugar. My phone was connected to the kitchen's speaker system, so the ring would be loud enough for me to hear in the garden. Cigarette, lighter, fresh tea in hand I ventured outside, where trace amounts of Otis Redding could find me and blend with birdsong. I looked back into the kitchen, though, and caught a glimpse of my reflection in the windowpane there. My curls hadn't yet been tamed by a hairbrush nor my bags filled in with foundation, or cosmetic concrete. But I wondered whether it was necessary, even, for a sit-down conversation with an employee; a would-be employee. Did I need to look perfect so I could sit opposite her and give her a rundown of my most imperfect experiences? I snorted at the thought, and a small puff of smoke rushed through my nose and scratched my throat all at once. My lungs struggled while I coughed away the amusement.

'That'll teach me to make myself laugh,' I said to a nearby blackbird, pecking furiously at a food tray that would need to be topped up again by late morning. 'Everyone is always so greedy around here.' I smiled and took another thirsty inhale of smoke. The neighbours were mostly quiet but in a small village everyone knew everything – or at least they thought they did. But they were always hungry for more. I wondered whether anyone would notice my visitor later in the day – whether anyone would catch her for a chat, even. The blackbird chirruped as I turned back from exhaling smoke away from him. He tilted his head, stared at me and chirruped once more. 'Everyone is chatty around here, too, aren't they?' I asked but he said nothing that time.

I ran a hand through my tangled mess of hair, swallowed tea and smoke again, and leaned back against the outer wall of home. The garden had taken a lot of work but it was a beautiful space in these early hours. From here, I could see straight down to the bottom; the neat grass and the encroaching shrubs and the birds that bounced from one side to the other. No one overlooked the garden, though, and that was perhaps my favourite thing about it. I listened hard to the birds outside, the opening chords of 'Hotel California', and the crackle of my cigarette burning down from another slow drag. Not for the first time, then, I wondered why I wanted to tell my story at all. In those quiet moments, with nothing to bother or threaten me, why now?

'Why does it matter anymore?'

The soft guitar drifting out from the kitchen was undercut by a kerfuffle, somewhere beyond the garden. I heard birds still, but behind the crunch of gravel. Then I lost them entirely to the shrill ring of my mobile through the speaker inside – only one ring, though, as requested. I asked her to let me know when she'd pulled up. I didn't rush the last of my cigarette – only three decent drags left – and then I exhaled, inhaled, exhaled as though the last of the smoke were the clearest air anyone might taste. I tried to laugh again, then, but the sound got caught in my throat and I drowned it with a drink.

Inside the kitchen the music was louder still but soft, soothing. Only the streaming service that I used always pulled the covers before the classics so I didn't recognise the singer behind this version. I was a child when the original track came out. Roger always played it; over and again whenever he was upset. Strange, then, that the song always stirred a fondness in me. I turned it off on my way to answer the door though. I was so worried of giving away clues.

# CHAPTER TWO

I didn't try to disguise my appearance.

The woman, who had disturbed the solitude of country living with a car that looked like it had never left the city before, was glancing around my open porchway. There were climbing vines and bursts of colour in full bloom, and she was framed like something from a fairy tale. I watched her for a second through the misted pane in the front door. But I knew I was unlikely to get away with that for long. When she turned her head to catch sight or smell of something nearby, her light blonde hair tumbled in the wind. It was a bob, short and neat but thick, too, in a way that must be nice to run a hand through. I yanked open the door then to halt any more thoughts, and the abruptness of the action startled her.

Still, she started the conversation with a laugh and an outstretched hand. 'Ruby?'

I matched the gesture. 'Prudence?'

'Oh.' She waved the name away. 'Call me Prue.'

*So that answers that one,* I thought as I stepped aside and made way for her to move through the front door. 'I'm sorry to have made you jump out here. Don't stand on the threshold.

Come in. I'll make us tea.' I closed the door and retraced my steps along the hallway, toward the kitchen. 'Unless you'd prefer coffee.'

'Tea would be great, thank you.' She had that faraway tone that comes with distraction. Without looking behind me, I guessed that she was sizing up the place on her walk through it, pausing, even, to stare at pictures pinned to the uneven walls. 'Could I have a glass of water, too, please? It's been so stuffy on that journey.'

'I can imagine.' I couldn't, though, because I couldn't remember the last time I'd allowed myself the luxury of a long journey anywhere. 'You're welcome to a walk down into the garden, if you'd like to stretch your legs.'

Prue craned to look out of the kitchen window then said, 'Ah, you're a smoker?'

'One a day, first thing.' The kettle started to hiss and steam while I ferreted out a clean cup, saucers, accompaniments. 'Do you have a preference on biscuits?'

'Anything with sugar.' She laughed again then, and I wondered whether she was nervous. *But she must have done this sort of thing before?* 'May I?' She gestured to the closed door that would lead her outside and I nodded.

I didn't like having to repeat myself. But still I answered. 'Please do.'

When I walked outside minutes later – laden with a tea tray that hadn't been used for years, on account of the lack of company – Prue was sat at the small dining set in a patch of shade. I lowered the tray and moved a free chair round to a spot of sun before sitting.

'You're a sun worshipper?' she asked.

'It helps my old bones.' I lifted the teapot. 'Say when.'

With drinks poured and cooling, we fell into the awkward silence that often swells between people who don't know each other, and who don't know where to begin. Prue filled the space by taking a greedy mouthful of tea followed by a biscuit that I suspect she only ate from politeness. But her quiet demeanour around each act made me wonder whether she thought she already knew something about me...

'You must have done this before?' I said eventually. 'Met someone, to talk through...'

She nodded. 'I have. But I'm also aware this is a very personal project to you and I'm more than happy for you to take the lead on what I do and don't know at this point. Counter to that, though, if you have any questions at all for me then I'm an open book when it comes to these things.' She reached for the slim satchel on the floor near her feet. 'I've brought my portfolio, which is an expanded version of the one available on the agency website, so you can fully browse past materials, too.' She'd slipped into business mode; her tone a different one now to the one she'd used inside the kitchen. When she finished speaking she flashed me a thin smile, then hurried to free her laptop.

'A very personal project,' I parroted. 'What makes you assume that?'

She looked up. 'I've been a ghost-writer for ten years and I've never had to sign two non-disclosure agreements ahead of even meeting the client.' Her smile loosened from the tight face she'd made before. 'It must be something quite personal, for that.'

I decided I liked her then.

'You've written books before?' I poured my own tea.

'Mostly fiction. My non-fiction usually deals with content writing work more so than memoirs or biographies. Although I've done them both before, but on a smaller scale to what I think you've requested.'

'I want a full manuscript.'

'Then that's what you'll get.' She took another biscuit. 'If you decide to work with me.'

Prue opened the laptop and speedily typed in what I assumed must be her password. I let the quiet sit between us while she readied things. The sun, already making its way around the garden now, was nearly out of my reach. I was glad of the opportunity to lean forwards into the shifting rays, under the guise of seeing her computer screen.

'I can give you copies of these, if you'd like to look through them in more detail.' She leaned back and sipped her tea while I skimmed the titles of her works.

'This is quite a list.'

'I'm quite a writer.' Her tone was relaxed.

Prue's hair caught in a sudden burst of wind and I noticed the thickness of it again; signs of her health, her youth. Although she spoke like a seasoned professional in her career, which made it impossible to guess her age. If she hadn't shown me her timeline of works, I would have assumed I had twenty years on her.

'Are you married?' Her relaxed expression faltered then, and I could see she was thrown by the question. I laughed. 'Sorry, it's not my business. I was trying to work out your age from your stress signs and knowing whether you were married might help.' I didn't mind admitting the truth behind my questioning. I'd spent such a long time answering questions in half-honesty, but these days I moved through the desire to pull the wool over people, or wrap it around them. I was of an age when confessing everything didn't seem fearsome anymore. Still, I added, 'You don't have to answer.'

She took the laptop back; clicked and scrolled and clicked. 'No, I'm not married.' She turned the machine back to me, and smiled. 'No spouse, no children, although I do have a cat who I call my child and I believe that's the closest I'll get to birthing anything. I don't have family; I did, of course, but now I don't. I misplaced them.' She forced a laugh but I wondered what the comment might be hiding. 'I've been with the same agency of writers on and off since I left university, where I studied English literature with creative writing. Hence,' she gestured to the laptop, 'the never-ending portfolio. I haven't always wanted to be a ghost-writer, but it gives me a good chance to work on lots of different projects which I do enjoy, and it pays the bills well enough for me to work on my own writing. Fiction, crime.' She dropped back heavily in her chair and fanned her hands as though presenting something. *There you have it*, her gesture said.

'You're a crime writer?'

She raised a finger. 'I hope to be.'

'Detective work?'

'Part detective, part... I don't know. Something psychological.'

'I'm hooked.'

She laughed. 'If only it were that easy.'

'Have you worked on crime reporting before, in content writing?'

I flickered in and out of listening to her answer. The sun had moved further out of reach and I looked up to scowl at its unwillingness to keep me warm. In the middle of her lengthy response, Prue commented she didn't follow crime reporting in real time and I wondered whether that was why she was still using my fake name; maybe she really didn't know. Initially it had felt like the most sensible decision to keep myself secreted away for this first meeting. But I wondered, then, whether life would have been easier had she known from the start; she would have walked through the door with her eyes open, rather than squinting.

'But enough about me,' she said. She slapped her thighs and

leaned in to close the gap between us. The breeze carried her perfume across to me. It was something like peaches, and summer. 'What do I need to know about you, Ruby?'

I took a deep breath and felt my chest pull at the action. 'About me, or the project?'

'Both, but you can decide the order of importance.'

'I don't know that there's much about me to share these days.'

'You're... retired?' she asked, guessing, too, at my age.

'I inherited some money about fifteen years ago. My father passed away and left me – well, left me everything. I was his only surviving relative, which meant I got the property and the money. I sold off the former, spent wisely with the latter, and I've been quietly living out my days here since then.'

Prue reached into the bag and pulled out a notebook. 'Do you mind?'

'Not at all.'

She flicked to a fresh page and made a note of something. 'No family?'

The question stung. 'No. No, it's only me.'

'You're not married either then.'

Instinctively, my right hand closed in around my left and I fingered the slight indent where the ring had been. It was years ago when I'd removed the gold loop, but somehow the skin had never felt the same.

'I was.'

'Divorced?' She didn't even look up; she must have been so sure of the answer. In fact, I thought she was already midway through writing the word when my response came.

'Widowed.'

Her face was troubled when she looked up. 'I'm so sorry, Ruby.'

'It was a long time ago.'

'Do you mind if I ask…'

This time when I inhaled there was a pain rather than a pull. I couldn't tell whether it was the action or the anxiety that had caused it. But I tried to slow the outbreath enough to steady my reply. 'He was murdered.'

Prue's eyes stretched at the word, then narrowed. 'That's what the book is about.'

*Clever girl.* I nodded. 'Yes, loosely, that's what I'd like the book to be about.'

She closed her notebook and set it on the table in front of her, then folded her hands in her lap. The expression she wore was soft, somehow. It had been a long time since anyone had looked at me in that way. In the village I was known, yes; meaning people knew that I existed. But beyond the moniker, the occasional half pint of shandy, and the early morning walk for the weekend newspaper, people didn't know me that well. It wasn't a criticism of them though; they did try to suck me into village life when I'd first bought the cottage. But the lack of neighbours had been part of the place's appeal. Though the isolation wore thin now and then. During those times, I reminded myself that this was exactly what I'd wanted – until now.

'You want to know what happened.'

'If I'm going to write about it, then…' She petered out.

'Of course.' I topped up my cold tea with what was left of the milk. 'He went missing for a short while, during which time there was a search. His body was discovered. There was a trial. The suspect was found not guilty. And now we're here.'

She looked startled. 'There are a lot of blanks in that.'

'Yes.' I glanced away from her. The sensation of being seen, studied, suddenly made me uncomfortable. 'I suppose that's what the project is for, to fill in the blanks.'

'You said there was a trial, a suspect?'

'Quite a lengthy one. There was a lot about it in the papers at the time, too.' I swallowed the beginnings of a laugh. 'And occasionally for the anniversaries of it all.' The media hadn't been especially good at leaving my husband alone during the aftermath of his death, and they'd made a meal of him since. There were documentaries, whole fandoms, my solicitor had told me; with half of the clingers-on believing one conspiracy and half of them fabricating others. Everyone loved a mystery, though, and the unsolved murder of a middle-class man in rural England had given the bloodhounds a taste of something worth reporting – re-reporting.

Prue grabbed the notebook again. I watched her slip easily back into professional mode. 'Would it be okay for me to take your husband's name?'

'Roger Miller.'

There was a long delay between my saying his name and her looking up. She hadn't written anything down. And I imagined how, in the seconds that had passed, her brain must have connected the dots and formed a watercolour. She opened her mouth twice before anything emerged; first, just a noise before it could form fully as a word. The side of my mouth twitched but I did my utmost to level out the smile that was forming. I knew how it would look. Instead, I sat passive and waited for Prue to decide what happened next.

'Roger Miller,' she repeated then took another pause, and a breath so deep that I worried there'd hardly be enough air left in the garden for me. 'Which must mean the suspect in the trial was–'

'Me.'

# CHAPTER THREE

I didn't ask for an answer straight away.

Prue looked young enough to have a loose knowledge of the case. But not old enough to know how it unfolded in real time. She'd asked what had happened and I'd told her a potted version, including police interviews and a brief stint in the cells. Then I told her how it was reported on by the media. My life and Roger's death became a growing tumour of inaccuracies – and somehow I always came off the worse.

'That's why you want to write the book?' she'd asked, and I'd nodded. 'Why now?'

I'd stood from the rickety chair then. When I pulled in the cool air, the sound of my chest matched that of the rusted joints in the table set and I knew it was time to move indoors. 'We'll come to that.'

After an overly polite farewell Prue trod back towards her car. I watched from the porchway and tried to see whether there was anything nervous in her step. I didn't rightly know what I was looking for. But when she turned back and waved me an additional goodbye, I at least believed we were leaving things on good terms. Although she was a smart girl; maybe she'd thought far enough ahead and decided she simply didn't want to be on bad terms with a monster. *Accused monster*, I'd corrected myself as I matched her wave. She'd thrown her bag on the passenger seat and slammed the door, and that's when I shouted.

'Prue, remember this is entirely your decision, won't you?'

She made a pained expression but said, 'Of course, Ru– Eri–'

'Erica. When it's just us, Erica is fine.' I'd smiled and she'd tried to match it, but it looked awkward on her.

Colin had warned me what a risk this might be. When I'd told him what my plans were around idle chit-chat, last wills, and NDAs; he'd cautioned me against exposing myself after years of closed-off comfort. But I'd stressed the need for it, as much as he'd then stressed the need for the paperwork. I hadn't wanted to be obvious, though, when I reminded Prue what was at stake for her. Still, I added, 'You've got a copy of the paperwork for this meeting, haven't you? All of the paperwork?'

From her face I could see she'd slipped back into professional mode. She didn't go as far as verbally answering, though, and instead thinned her lips, nodded and gave me a theatrical salute – as though obeying orders. And I'd liked that...

At the edge of my driveway there were two rabbits mating. I needed milk, but I felt rude disturbing them. The courtship had taken longer than usual and the male, after trying quite so hard, at least deserved his moment. I flitted between watching and trying not to watch until they were finished. Even after they'd gone, it took me a minute to tear myself away from the ghost of their intimacy, marked in the dishevelled gravel kicked up by their scrambling feet. I sighed and looked at the cigarettes on the windowsill. *One a day, that's the deal*, I reminded myself before I dropped my cup into the sink and grabbed a cardigan.

Outside, the sun was out but the trees and their leaves were flustered by a breeze. The weather hadn't warmed up, although the news had said it was supposed to. The walk from the cottage to the main village was an exposed one, too, made up of open fields and hedgerows. There wasn't much to shield me from the winds until I got into the village proper, where more cottages started to appear; one here and one there at random intervals as though they were self-seeding. The wind, slowed now, wasn't quite loud enough to cover the creak of curtains pulling back; locals peering from their dusty windows to see who was roaming through their land. It had taken me a long time to integrate myself since I'd moved in. Though there was a fine line to tread between making sure people were interested enough to say hello, but not so interested that they might google your name. If any of them had ever been moved to look into Ruby Brinkley, they would have soon realised I wasn't her.

'Morning, Mrs Brinkley.'

*Ms.* I turned and smiled before I even knew who it was; it was my default reaction. 'Joey!' A young boy, all blushed cheeks and bushy hair, was perched on his bicycle but peering out from under a helmet that fit him like a hand-me-down. 'Are you well?'

'Yes, Mrs Brinkley, fit and well. I've been riding. I'm getting quite good at going down the Gregory Hillside now. I think I'll be able to catch my brothers up soon.' He spoke at such a speed the words knocked into each other, one tyre chasing the next. 'Are you well, Mrs–'

'Fit and well myself, Joey, fit and well.' I carried on walking. Though he answered, the breeze carried his words away. I only shouted back, 'I'll be seeing you,' then I kept on along my way until I arrived outside of the village shop. It was manned by two older ladies, Edna and Bessie, who had retired here; a non-couple, though I'd seen how they were together and I recognised a lie when I saw one. The two of them were huddled when I walked in; not suspiciously close, though, as one craned over the shoulder of the other, to help aging eyes read the small print of something. They looked up and smiled when they saw me. It had always felt like there was something unspoken between the three of us, as though they could sense I, too, was living a secret.

'Morning, Ruby.'

'Ladies.'

I trod around to the fridge at the back. My hand hovered between the smaller and medium measurements and a tremor of something moved through my fingers. *It's only you. How much milk can one woman need?* I forced out a long exhale, clenched and unclenched my fingers, then chose the smaller option.

'Nothing else?'

'Nothing else.' I counted out the exact money. 'Have a good day, ladies.'

They smiled in unison. But then Edna said, 'Visitor yesterday?'

But of course, no one missed a trick. 'A friend.'

'Young friend. We thought it might be your daughter,' Bessie added.

*No, still barren.* 'I don't have children,' I said flatly, although they were beyond the age to feel embarrassed. 'She's just a friend from the city.'

Edna opened her mouth but Bessie paused her with a raised hand. 'Ruby's got better things to do than stand around here and be interrogated. Haven't you, dear?'

I forced a laugh. 'And here I thought my days of being interrogated were behind me.'

'Oh, well now–'

'Edna,' Bessie cut her off. 'Give it a rest and get back to your reading.'

'Always a pleasure, ladies,' I said and then made for the door before their sniping could spill out into a mess larger than it needed to be. I'd seen their fond looks, swapped when they thought no one was paying attention. But I'd also heard them have a spat before, too, and it was nothing that I longed to be a part of.

On the walk home no one at all bothered me. Of course, that's not to be confused with no one at all seeing me. I wondered how many other people had noticed Prue's visit; not that it mattered, particularly if it was a singular occurrence. Still, I checked my watch then, and thought back to our agreement – 'Get in touch if you want the job, and if you don't then I'll know.' – and the days that had elapsed since. Colin would be able to contact another agency; another agency would send another writer. It would become Chinese whispers, though, on who could hold their tongue the longest. Though I wouldn't admit as much to Colin, since meeting Prue I had felt uncomfortably aware of how big a risk the endeavour to share my story might be. I pulled in cool air, forced it out in a longer breath, and reminded myself that this was what the non-disclosure agreement was for.

When I rounded the corner onto my driveway there was a rabbit, only one now, waiting.

'Are you the lover or the loved?' I asked but it bolted before answering.

I fumbled with my key in the front door; flicked the kettle to boil and again eyed my cigarettes before checking my phone, left on the table. The run-through felt like a hierarchy of what mattered these days. But when I pressed the home button on my handset, I saw there was a voicemail from a withheld number – which Colin seldom ever used, knowing that I wouldn't answer.

'You have one new message...' I pressed three and waited.

'Miss Miller, it's Prue, Prudence Carr, from the agency.' There was a long pause then. 'I've given your job some thought.' Another long pause. I readied myself for a blunt rejection. But instead she said, 'I'll do it.'

# CHAPTER FOUR

I didn't have many ground rules.

Prue sent me her own terms and conditions when we agreed to work together. It was nothing official – nothing I had to sign, that is – but an outline of how she typically worked. She sent it in advance of our first official meeting, and I printed it off the evening before she was due to arrive. The living room smelt of cinnamon and fire; I lowered the sound on the radio to listen to the crackle of the flames as I read her bullet points. Roger had always hated an open fire. He told me more than once how dangerous they were and I told him, as many times, fire was only dangerous if you were careless enough to get burned. *Which I never had been*, I thought as I tucked my legs beneath me, with something like melancholy; nostalgia curled itself up into a ball by my feet. There were times when I missed him so much the feeling was tangible, and I could imagine it as a pet – or an unwanted rodent.

I reached for the squat glass of red wine next to me, took a generous sip, and read. Prue's points were written in clusters according to different headings. Initially, they looked to be about her working hours. Then, they moved into her process.

She took Sundays off, according to her hymn sheet, but she didn't mind working evenings and Saturdays to suit a client's needs. I was two thirds of the way down the first of two pages when I flung the papers to one side, drank another sip of wine and rested my head against the back of the sofa. It hadn't been a long day, I didn't think, and yet the tiredness...

A harsh laugh bubbled out. 'It's been a long twenty years, though, hasn't it?'

Before tiredness could claim me, then, I decided to read the rest of Prue's conditions. There was nothing especially demanding in any of it, though, only a writer who wanted (difficult) clients to know what she would and wouldn't tolerate as part of her employment – and I found that I liked her more for that. I reached across to the other end of the side table to grab a pen and felt a stab of pain in my side as I moved; a twinge, like something twisting. So instead of the pen I brought back the glass of wine and took another mouthful, then another. When the wine was only a stain in the bottom of the crystal, I reached again for the pen and my body felt more successful on this second attempt.

In the last of the fire's light, I flipped over Prue's rule sheet and wrote my own.

---

Prue arrived five minutes before her due time, but she waited in the car until one minute to. When she climbed out, she brought with her the same bag as before and a smile that looked only the slightest bit nervous. *She'll have done research by now*, I thought as I waved to her from the kitchen window. I crossed out of sight to the front door when she spotted me, and I opened it just as she arrived in the porch.

'Come on in, get yourself settled and comfortable.'

She held the bag against her chest like a shield. 'Where is best to work?'

'Do you need a back support?'

'I'm sorry?'

I laughed. 'Of course, you aren't as ancient as I am so maybe you don't need to think about these things.' I started to walk to the kitchen and she dutifully followed. 'If you need a back support then we can work here, or at the dining table. If you don't then we can work in the living room on a sofa apiece. Hot or cold drink?'

Prue looked flustered but said, 'Cold, please. Can we–'

'Lemonade?'

'Perfect.' She waited until I was busying myself, then asked, 'How about outside?'

*It's not warm enough out there for me today.* 'Terrible noise from the surrounding fields today,' I lied. 'Some harvest or another. Maybe next time, though, we can spend some time out there. We can find you a spot of shade and I'll sun worship.' Her skin was paler today than it had been before and I wondered whether it was cosmetic, or whether something was wrong. I opened my mouth to ask but, *boundaries, dear,* I reminded myself. 'Back support?' She smiled, shook her head and flashed a frustrated-sympathetic-confused look that you might typically reserve for an elderly relative. I liked her less then. 'Why don't you go and pick a sofa?'

When I followed her in some minutes later – laden with tea, lemonade, biscuits – she'd picked the sofa opposite my own. I was glad she hadn't claimed my space. I lowered the tray to the coffee table between us and took up my own perch with my legs tucked beneath me again, and a soft throw covering me. I felt like a small child at story time.

'Did you have the chance to look over the document I sent?' she asked.

'I did. No objections there on my part. It's very conscientious of you, to have a list like that ready and waiting for new clients.'

'Ruby, I could tell you some horror stories about–'

'Erica.'

She clenched her eyes closed. 'I'm sorry, Erica. Can I– can I ask why Ruby?'

I fidgeted, readjusted my legs and sighed. It was impossible to get them comfortable sometimes. 'I came here to start afresh. I already looked different, older. No one recognised me.'

'From the news?'

'The news. The papers. Even the internet. My face was everywhere for a while.'

'It must have been so difficult.' She sounded sincere. But whether she was or not, I didn't want her sympathy. I'd given myself more than enough of that over the years.

'Still, I can set the record straight now.'

She was midway through starting up her laptop but my comment stopped her in her tracks. 'Erica, I realise this is your project, and your life,' she nearly laughed, 'but are you sure that you want to do this?' She didn't wait for me to answer before she carried on with her unpacking. The next thing to be pulled from her Mary Poppins bag of tricks was a voice recorder which she set down between us.

'I don't want anything recorded.'

She looked across to me then. 'Nothing at all?'

'Everything can be written, note form or however suits you best. But I don't want anything recorded.' Prue looked like she was about to argue her case, so I added, 'I have my terms and conditions as well.'

She slipped the recorder out of sight. 'Very well. Let's hear them.' She dropped her hands in her lap and waited with a playful smile.

'I don't want you to do any research.'

And the smile dropped.

'Nothing at all?'

'Nothing beyond what I give you.' She looked ready to argue again and I felt a stab of dislike. It was a very Roger thing, for her to be looking for arguments. 'The book isn't about the information that's already available, Prue.' I leaned forward and took a sip of my drink, and she won back a Brownie point by waiting. 'If I wanted a book that's about the information already available, I'd look to the heinous amounts of biographies and transcripts and podcasts and – God, however many other productions there are about me, about Roger. There's a wealth of crap, pardon my language, but utter crap about what happened, about what I apparently did. The book is about what I didn't do; the things they've told everyone that I did, but I didn't.'

I couldn't decide whether I wanted to turn over the table with rage or sink back into the sofa with sadness.

'I can understand, Erica.'

*No, you can't.* I pulled in a big breath and forced a smile. *But you will.*

'If there are points that I need to research then I won't press forward with it before asking you. I'm thinking of things like who was the editor of a certain paper or...' She paused and felt around for another example. I nodded, though, to let her know she'd made her case. 'I won't research you personally, or Roger.'

'Thank you.'

'All in a day's work.' She smiled. If we'd been close enough for contact, I would have leaned over to squeeze her hand. 'Is there anything else?'

'We'll never do two days in a row of talking. It will be too much for us both.' I had no idea whether it would be too much for Prue but she was polite enough to nod along like she agreed.

I knew it would be too much for me – and that was all that mattered. There would need to be recuperation time between each meeting, and there were appointments outside of my time with Prue to juggle. 'Do you have other work commitments?' I asked, feeling around to add credence.

'I only do one long-form project at a time,' she admitted and she sounded disappointed in herself. 'But if I'm writing everything in note form and then typing it up, it will help to have a day or two here and there to make sure I can keep on top of that. May I?' She pointed to the untouched biscuits.

I'd only bought them for her visit. 'Please.'

She spoke around a mouthful of crumbs then. 'Next?'

I pressed my lips together and shrugged. 'No next.'

'Well,' she pulled a notebook free from her open bag, 'let's get started.'

With some effort I lowered my legs. 'Cramp,' I lied, but it bought me the time I needed to stand and steady myself. 'There are a few things over here that might be helpful.' I walked around to the slim stretch of space behind her sofa and grabbed a handle from the edge of a boxy chest. It was designed to look like a stack of books. Roger had bought it, thinking it a genius invention. I laughed at the memory. 'Roger bought this.'

She craned around to look. 'I love those things.'

I wasn't sure whether she was saying it to humour me, so I only smiled and carried on pulling at the weighty box. 'This thing is full of...' I didn't know what to call it other than detritus, but that seemed a strange thing to gift someone. 'Memorabilia.'

Prue opened the box like a child unwrapping a present they didn't feel deserving of. She took it slowly, with an obvious measure of suspicion, and angled herself to peer under the lid before she got it fully opened. *It won't bite*, I thought of saying but I didn't want to take the threat away. She was sitting in a room with an accused murderess; maybe she was right to be nervous. *Maybe it would be stranger still if she weren't nervous at all...*

I landed heavily on the sofa alongside her and waited for her to pull the first item out. She eyed up a hefty ledger with *THE SUN AND STAR* written in block capitals across the front.

'The newspaper?' she asked, only she didn't seem concerned with my answer. Prue pulled the pages apart, a puppy at Christmastime, and I wondered whether she would rip through them. But as a realisation rose up through her she slowed down. I thought of asking her whether she felt okay but I didn't want to interrupt the moment. Instead I leaned in, as though stretching to see what page she was on; really, though, I only wanted the closeness. I thought she even pressed back against me, a little, when my thigh was against her own. 'These are... scrapbooks?' She moved the open folder to one side and started to rifle through the others. She didn't lift them from the chest, though, only skimmed their titles then pushed down to the next. 'Is this– These folders, they're everything they wrote about you?'

I turned a page in the folder she'd discarded, read a headline – "Miller murderess makes claim to fortune" – and smiled. There was a lot from that time that had faded. But there was certain slander that stuck. The day this had been printed was the day after another newspaper had run a feature on whether Roger had life insurance (he didn't) alongside a chronological list of noughties' killers who had been motivated by such a thing. Still, the articles were picked up and passed on, then they landed in the laps of people who had heard from another source... And somehow, then, I became the woman who murdered her husband for money. It was one of many motives the media suggested, though, and certainly not the most original of the bunch.

I closed the book, to pull back my concentration on the task at hand.

'This is everything.' Prue looked startled and I thought she needed comfort, then, at the velocity of the project. But she was being paid hard cash for the privilege of rifling through these unmentionables, so that assuaged me from any guilt. 'Well,' I broke the barrier of contact and reached over to grab her hand, then, 'everything, that is, except all the things I *did* do.'

# CHAPTER FIVE

I didn't expect to like her quite so much.

Prue was a beautiful woman. After I handed over the chest to her – 'Here, browse through it as much as you'd like.' – I moved back to my own sofa opposite, thereby giving me a good viewpoint. Funny, how quickly I came to think of the sofa as hers after only seeing her settled in it once. She was the only other person who had ever nested in the living room with me, though, and I assumed the emotional pulls I felt towards her could be put down to that. Whenever Colin visited we would sit at the kitchen table, or in the dining room depending on the amount of paperwork he'd brought. We'd socialised only once, in the garden. The living room, then, was an uncluttered space – or it had been, until Prue.

I watched as she pored over each ledger in detail. She'd been there for nearly two hours when she came up for air. She shook her head and her hair tumbled around her face; then she ran a hand through it to clear it from her eyes. Prue looked like the sort of woman to use conditioning products. I wondered how soft it would be, whether my fingers would find tangles or whether they'd move right through it. Her eyes looked tired; I could imagine her wearing reading glasses, late into the night during hours of heavy research.

'Do you wear spectacles?'

She laughed. 'To drive. I should wear them when I work sometimes, I think.' She rubbed at her eyes. 'Do you mind if I use your bathroom?'

'Please do. Hallway, stairs, first door on the right when you reach the landing.' She didn't move, though, despite the directions, and I sensed there was more. There was something like worry sitting next to her; a neat creature that I wanted to reach over and soothe. 'Are you okay, Prue?'

'How did you cope with this?'

'I'll need a little more.' I smiled. 'Losing Roger?'

'Losing Roger. Being accused of...' She gestured to the folders. 'Everything.'

When I initially discussed plans for a memoir with Colin, he hadn't asked why; I suppose he'd known me for long enough to understand. But he had warned me that anything already printed could be dredged up; anything that hadn't been talked about the first time around would likely need to be, now. He'd warned me, too, that anyone in their right mind would have reservations about spending hours, days at a time locked up in a cottage, without a neighbour in shouting distance, with an accused murderer. I'd laughed and said that perhaps everyone wasn't as squeamish as him, but he hadn't shared in my humour. 'I mean it, Erica,' he'd said, 'people will be wary.' But Prue didn't seem to be. Instead, she showed only sympathy at the sheer volume of texts published about what remained the worst thing ever to happen in my life. Losing a spouse is traumatic enough but having people Rubik's Cube the riddle of whether you murdered them was a trauma too far.

And that was another thing I liked about Prue: she hadn't asked...

'I was close to my father,' I answered, 'and he was a great support throughout it all.'

'He's who the inheritance money came from?' The question winded me and she rushed to apologise. 'Erica, I'm sorry that was–'

'Don't. There's no polite way of asking questions like that but you'll need to know.' I paused to cough and felt the splash of something inside my chest. 'Yes, he's where the inheritance came from. He was a successful man and I was an only child.'

'Your mother is...'

I waved away the line of enquiry. 'We'll come to that. For now, you need the bathroom and I need more tea.'

'Of course.' She smiled, stood and made for the doorway, but she lingered on the boundary of the room. 'Erica, the ledgers, could I take th–'

'No.'

She sighed and it struck me how clear the sound was; how healthy. I liked her a little less for a minute or two then.

It was important to keep eating; I knew that as a biological truth. But in the lonely hours of a Sunday afternoon, I couldn't muster the energy to move to the kitchen and create. The prospect of walking to the village felt easier, somehow; the thought of the fresh air and country sounds along the route. It was a sunny day, too, so I pulled a cardigan around me and packed a bag: notebook; pen; paperback; purse. My mobile hummed with a shrill tone that made me flinch and, after seeing it was Colin calling, I decided to leave it behind.

'Not even Prue works on a Sunday,' I said, then I turned the handset screen down and left. I wasn't sure why she'd become my benchmark for things. But on the walk along my driveway, down to the road that ran along the outskirts of my land, I wondered how she spent her Sundays. It occurred to me in a rapid two-step process that: I could call her to invite her to have lunch with me; that would be wildly inappropriate. I paused, leaned on a nearby post and pulled air in, pushed it back out, felt the sensation of something crackling on my inside. *I should have brought a second cardigan.* But I didn't trust that going back wouldn't also mean calling Prue.

In the distance a noise like a gunshot rang out. 'Get off, get off with you, bloody rat.'

I took it as a sign to carry on walking. Although the sun was shining, the air itself had the cool crispness that usually belonged to early mornings; somehow it had leaked into the rest of the day. It made deep breaths sting but there was something fresh about the feeling, too, and I imagined how the air might be sweeping clean my insides. Along the way there was the rustle of greenery as surrounding life scarpered, like it always seemed to. And I thought of Roger then. I carried the thoughts right into the village. He would have loved to live somewhere like this; curtain twitching and quiet was his retirement plan. He, too, would have preferred a lazy Sunday afternoon spent sitting outside a pub rather than sweating in a kitchen.

'Afternoon, Ruby.' The voice snatched me from my thoughts. 'Where you heading?'

Hugh was, I wagered, the youngest adult in a five-mile radius; he was also the landlord of the pub. He was bent over a table, stacking empty pint glasses into each other.

'To you, actually.'

He looked up, then, and said, 'Unusual for you. Table for two, is it?'

*So they've seen Prue...* 'No, just one. Room for me?'

'Always. Were you hoping for the carvery though? Because that's long gone.' He turned without waiting for an answer and started to tread toward the door. But then added, 'Mind you, we can probably plate you up a few bits from things left?'

'Oh, would you?'

'Course.' He stood in the doorway and faced me. 'Are you in or out?'

Through the nearest window I could see an empty table. 'Window seat?'

'Get yourself settled. Glass of red?'

'I'm predictable?' I joked and he smiled.

'I'm just good at my job.'

Hugh went back to cleaning up, and I seated myself at the table in quiet. There was an empty chair facing off against me and I wondered what it might be like to have these excursions with company. *Perhaps I will ask her, one week*, I thought. I wondered what Prue might drink. She'd likely order something non-alcoholic; a lemonade with a squeeze of lime had been her preferred drink when we were together. Outside of work, though, she might be inclined to something else. She didn't have the blush of a frequent drinker; she was too young for that. But there was a chance she might take a taste of something alcoholic. She'd never commented on my red wine, though, so perhaps white. Or gin. I was assuming gin was still fashionable. Although if she did have something to drink then she'd need to stay for the whole evening; the country roads were lethal at the best of times and if she were to tackle them after a large gin and tonic, well, something might happen to her and then–

'I made it a large glass, as it's Sunday.'

Hugh cut the thought off and I was glad of it. 'You'll get me drunk.'

'Maybe that's my intention.' He winked, but his tone was jovial.

'Oh, you wouldn't need to get me drunk, Hugh. Only ask nicely.'

'Well, if it's a case of asking nicely for things,' he rested his hands on the edge of my table, 'who's the young woman who's been visiting you these past few days?'

I leaned forward and lowered my voice. 'The old ones are rubbing off on you.'

He laughed and asked, 'Maybe I'm just thinking of asking the lady if she'd like a drink here, ever think of that?'

I hadn't thought of it. But I didn't like it. 'She's not single.' The lie rushed out.

'Oh. Oh, I think I see.'

*What do you see?* I imagined a pot of monies sitting behind the bar with a notebook alongside it. Were they placing bets? Did they wonder whether Prue was a lover? Perhaps it hadn't crossed Hugh's mind at all until he'd asked; perhaps I'd thrown an unconsidered option into the listings. *Will you add that now, Hugh, claim the thought as your own?* But the older villagers would dismiss it, surely. Then, I wondered how far down the list they'd written the word "daughter". Had that been one of the first suggestions? I'd never mentioned a husband nor partner; who would I have mentioned him to? Still, that may have only added to the intrigue of Prue. The possibilities of her role rushed around my mind, creating such a knock-on knock-on knock... I hadn't even noticed Hugh speak.

'Ruby?'

'I'm sorry?' I blinked away the ideas.

'I said, did I just accidentally hit on your daughter?' His face relaxed into a smile and I tried to match the expression.

'What makes you think she's my daughter?'

'Well, she could be a lover. But that would make you quite a dark horse, Ruby.'

'Hugh,' I laughed along with him, 'I'm a wild mare if only you all realised.'

He let the matter go then, although he laughed all the way

to the bar. After, I tried to focus on the world outside of the window. But I carried Hugh's suggestions with me, swaddled in my own feral thoughts of Prue as a child. Roger and I had talked about children – all married couples are forced to at some point – although we'd both agreed we enjoyed life too much as it was to introduce a child into it. Still, in idle hours alone now, I found that I kept thinking: of Prue; of the children I didn't have; of the child I'd flushed away.

# CHAPTER SIX

I didn't come from a poor background.

*The Telegraph* was spread apart on my kitchen table. I wasn't in the habit of reading newspapers – I found them triggering – but Colin had left it behind two days ago and I reasoned it mightn't hurt to find out what I was missing in the world. *Nothing much though,* I thought as I scanned another page. I'd left *The Herald* scrapbook on the coffee table in the living room in anticipation of Prue's arrival, too, and it irked me to feel so surrounded by media. She'd asked whether we could start at the beginning, when I was a child. I'd told her I didn't think my childhood made a difference to the book and she'd said, 'But don't you want everyone to know everything?'

I skimmed another page, licked my finger, turned. *Within reason.*

I cleared my throat and coughed up the taste of my cigarette. It crossed my mind that a second one might help. But it was a thought I had most days now. Instead, I folded the paper back into creases and squeezed myself free of the table. From the window I could see both the driveway and a good portion of the garden. Things were becoming overgrown out there and I wondered whether it was pathetic fallacy – but the herbaceous version. *Is there a phrase for that?* I ran a hand through my knotted hair and felt the barbs of grey that were drying out the colour. There was a young man in the next village over who'd pushed a card through once, boasting something about being young and fit enough to tend your garden for you. I'd been furious at the time but – I cast an eye around the kitchen, as though the card might be lying in plain sight – I'd still kept it for safekeeping. My past self had been more open-minded about how my stamina might change.

Before I could collapse into self-pity Prue rounded the corner into the driveway. The gravel cracked under the weight of her car, so loud that it moved through the windows, and I tried to remember the last proof of life in the world that I'd heard before that. *The newspaper's pages turning, of course,* I reminded myself, to steer away from catastrophising whatever feelings were brewing. *Ah, but that was a sound* I'd *made...* The car door slammed and Prue waved to catch my attention. I matched the gesture, waved back and felt a stab of pain somewhere in my ribs. She was looking into the passenger side of the car, though, so she missed the grimace and I'd been glad. When the other door was slammed shut, she started toward me. She didn't even go to the trouble of locking the car anymore; she felt so safe. Or she wanted to always be able to escape quickly.

She looked beautiful every day. A long black cardigan blew back behind her as she walked. It was criminal that there wasn't anyone waiting to take her picture. *Oh, but she'll be famous one day,* I reminded myself and smiled at the idea. She was wearing boots with a small heel that left indents along the gravel as she trod. She must have walked over hearts with those heels, or others like them. There was something about Prue that gave off that impression; that she might be one of those women who are impossible to love.

'Which makes her a clever girl,' I said quietly as the knock at the door came. 'Open!'

'You're ready for me,' she announced as she came to a stop in the doorway. I followed her stare to a tray on the sideboard, loaded with a squat jug of lemonade with ice. There was a small bowl of lime slices alongside it, and a fresh glass. 'Am I late?' She was already checking her watch.

'Not at all. I was ready early.'

'Everything okay?' she asked, in a tone that suggested she thought otherwise.

I nodded. 'Of course. Living room? I've had the fire going.'

'Perfect. It's quite chilly out there this morning.' She walked ahead of me.

'Roger always hated open fires, you know, said that someone would–'

'I remember you saying.' She laughed as she landed on her sofa.

I couldn't remember saying. But I didn't care for the interruption either way.

'I've left *The Herald* out. They were especially interested in who I was – before.'

She reached for the open book. 'Were they accurate?'

It was my turn to laugh. 'None of them were accurate, Prue.'

'Okay,' she dropped the book in her lap, 'so tell me your truth.'

'The truth,' I corrected her and flashed a tight smile. 'I had a very happy childhood with money and family and friends who liked me.'

'Have you ranked those things in order of importance?' Her tone was jovial.

Still, I answered honestly. 'Yes.'

'Money was the most important thing?'

'Isn't it to everyone?'

Her head twitched, but she didn't go as far as a shake. 'I suppose you need it to live.' She reached down to her bag and pulled out a notebook. 'What about Roger?' She uncapped her pen and turned to a fresh page. 'Was he geared towards money?'

'The older he got, the more important money was. But it wasn't always important.'

'What changed?'

'Oh, well that's an easy one.' I reached across to grab my blanket before I tucked my legs up and wedged my body so I was comfortable. 'When he was younger, he had none. When he got older, he did. Money is one of those things that has a tilting level of importance, I find, in accordance with how much you can get your hands on.'

'How did he come into money, if you don't mind me asking?' She was looking down at her notes, but her head snapped up when I answered.

'He got married.' I saw her glance at the newspaper clippings across the table then. 'Roger made some shoddy decisions when he was younger. But he didn't have much of a hand to guide him.' I waved the memories away. 'We'll come to that.'

'So, the papers,' she reached forward and tapped a scathing headline, 'they reported that you didn't have a good upbringing?'

'Some. Some said I didn't come from money. Some went as far to describe my upbringing as "rough", which I remember Dad having a good laugh over.' He was sick by then, though, so the laughter always sounded like a drain clogged with detritus. I thought it must have been how his chest looked too. 'I led a charmed life, Prue, that's the truth of it. I went to a good school and I had good friends, some were louder than others but I'm happy to believe you'd find that in most friendship circles?' I paused there and she laughed lightly, to confirm my suspicions.

'Dad funded my university years, because he could afford to, and I do realise how lucky that makes me, thank you very much...' I'd had enough people take a tone with me over the years. 'But there was nothing scandalous about where Dad's money came from either, which was another line some reporters went down.'

'But it's all fabricated?' There was a patch of redness spreading up from behind Prue's high-necked jumper. I wondered where the pink flesh started. 'This just isn't right, Erica, it isn't. I don't even understand how...' The more flustered she became the higher the red spread until it was touching the paleness of her face. 'People must know that this isn't true?'

'I suspect so.' I leaned forward to pour a glass of lemonade. 'But what's a girl to do?'

'You could have reported them, sued them, gone on the record with the...' She noted my raised eyebrow and then petered out of her rage. 'I'm sorry.'

'When all of this was happening, I was a little preoccupied.'

She opened her mouth as though to ask more but then snapped it closed quickly. I thought she'd been about to ask, before realising. 'Of course.'

'I think they were looking for a motive.'

'For Roger's death?'

I nodded. 'They knew he was dead by then. I was a suspect. I was–'

'An easy target.'

*We'll need to talk about these interruptions.* 'Yes, I suppose. They enjoyed making a monster.'

She laughed then; an abrupt noise that erupted like a belch. 'Erica, I've spent a handful of days with you and I can tell you already that I'd never describe you as monstrous.'

My own laugh emerged then, though it was deeper, harsher than Prue's. It caught on my throat and silenced me for a few seconds while I tried to swallow back whatever it had brought up. I chugged two mouthfuls of lemonade and focused on the fire, the warmth of it, all the while thinking what a terrible judge of character Prue was.

'Maybe we all have different ideas of monsters,' I said, though I wasn't looking at her.

'So what flavour of monster are you?'

I had to glance her way to check her expression. If I hadn't known better, I would have thought there was something flirtatious in her tone. But her face didn't give anything away.

'The poor kind, according to *The Herald*.' I didn't much feel like flirting, but I turned back to face her. 'Money was one of the things talked about a lot as part of the public trial. There were later reports,' I gestured to the box, 'that were more accurate about the money I'd come from. But that was a motive too. They assumed Roger had married me for my money and on discovering that I must have murdered him in a blind rage.'

'If you had that much money, wouldn't you have just paid someone?' she joked.

'Hush money is expensive.' Her face fell, so I winked to soften the comment and she laughed a little then. 'I went to Regent's Hall private school, before going to the University of York where I studied classics. You'll want to write that down because those names, specifically, were never listed anywhere and it's important that they are.' She followed instructions and I reasoned that I might be able to forgive her the earlier interruptions. 'The school was the best in the area at the time although I've no way of knowing whether it is now. Check?'

She nodded and made a note. 'The people you were at school with, they didn't help?'

'How so?'

'I don't know.' She shrugged. 'By telling the truth, saying they knew you.'

I laughed at the suggestion. The glug of my chest made me think of Dad again. 'We were raised to mind our own business and keep out of other people's. From a young age, that was all too apparent. It was written into the wills we inherited from.' Prue took the comment in good humour, but I wasn't being altogether hyperbolic. 'Besides, I didn't keep in touch with many school friends through the university years. You meet new people, don't you?'

Prue didn't look convinced. 'But you didn't have a *best* friend who might've helped?'

The comment winded me. My hands flew to my stomach as though Prue had struck a physical blow, and she leapt toward me when she noticed. 'I'm fine, I'm fine,' I lied so she slowly retreated. 'Cramps.' I was well beyond the age for a stomach cramp. She'd assume something else, though, I hoped, as I leaned back against the firm cushions behind me to let the sofa take my weight. I pushed air in and out until it didn't hurt anymore, and then I tried a laugh. 'I did have a best friend.'

'Are you okay?' she asked. Her worry looked real.

'Of course.' I waved the outcry away; I didn't want her knowing yet. 'This is an old body I'm wearing.' I took another deep breath to steady the waver in my voice. 'Yes, I did have a best friend. No, she wasn't in a position to help me.'

'Are you in touch now?'

I only shook my head.

'Okay,' her pen was ready, 'could I take her name? It might be helpful to—'

'Ruby.' Prue looked up then, and narrowed her eyes. 'Ruby Brinkley.'

'I see.' Her pen was still ready, as though expecting more. 'Would you have any objections to me reaching out to her? I wouldn't tell her about the project, at all, but it might be good to have other voices in the book.'

'Other than my own?'

'The odd quote never hurts, and it'll make you more human.' I laughed at her phrasing and the stomach pain flared but I tried not to let it show. 'I just mean, if you've got connections to the world, people who cared for you, who really knew you at the time. It might be worth having them on the record.'

'Well, we'll have to find someone else.' I lowered my legs. 'You'll have to excuse me for a minute.' I needed painkillers for whatever Prue had stirred. But I was only just about upright when she pushed another blow.

'Erica, I would really like to find her, I think– I truly believe it would help the book.'

'Someone else will have to make me more human then, Prue.' I started on my way out of the room, facing away from her as I spoke. 'Because you won't find Ruby Brinkley.'

# CHAPTER SEVEN

I didn't find myself in trouble from a young age.

Prue cancelled a meeting, which I didn't like. She did it by sending me a text message, too, which I liked even less. I'd always preferred to believe that people with her class had a better way of conducting themselves. But perhaps experience should have taught me the ignorance of that belief some time ago. Still, it came as a blow when she answered my follow-up phone call and feigned a migraine. *So why text*, I thought, *why inflict the agony of looking at a bright screen long enough to cancel our plans...* Instead, though, I forced sympathy and recommended a lie down in a darkened room. *Where you can think about what you've done...* Having shared so many years with Roger, I'd developed a nose for when headaches were and weren't faked. He and I had both used them in our time: to escape dinner with friends; to avoid visiting relatives; to cry off marital relations. I told her to take care and to let me know when she was feeling up to another meeting. There was a clause in our contract about the timescale of the project; I'd asked Colin to include it. So, she couldn't avoid me forever.

Not that she tried to. Instead, she arrived unannounced two days later.

'I wasn't expecting you.' I stood in the doorway, to signal that I wasn't going to allow an easy entry. I felt prickly towards her lie still, despite the easy smile she'd slapped on for now. 'Did we arrange for something?'

'No,' she shifted awkwardly, 'but this is when our next meeting should have been, I think? I had to take the day off, then a day's natural break, then a day back on it. So, that brings us to today. I'm sorry,' she looked past me into the hallway, 'is it a bad time?'

I stepped aside then, and forced a smile. 'I'm a little unkempt but come on in.'

'Oh, you look just fine to me.'

'Get yourself settled in the living room,' I said, ignoring the compliment. 'I'll make tea.' I waited for her to correct me and request her usual swill of lemonade, but she didn't. She only trod along the hallway and then ducked out of sight into the lounge. I'd been listening to The Eagles but the volume slowly died, and I wondered why Prue had presumed to turn it down. I assumed if she felt comfortable enough to turn my music down then she'd likely seen herself to the comfort of my sofa now too. Unless she was buried behind it with her head in the box of scrapbooks.

I held myself steady with hands gripped to the kitchen sideboard, and I waited for the kettle to boil. The sound of the water bubbles must have covered the sound of Prue walking into the room, though, so when I turned to pull an extra mug from the cupboard she made me jump with a ferocity that sent my chest reeling. 'Bollocks.'

'Erica.' She stepped close enough to set a hand on my shoulder. 'Shit, I'm sorry.'

I tried to remember the last time I'd been touched by

someone who wasn't a doctor. 'Don't be.' I smiled but pulled away from her. 'You caught me off guard.'

'Are you okay?'

'Of course, of course.' I waved away her concern. 'Guilty conscience.'

She took the comment in the spirit it was intended and laughed along. But when I looked at her there was something hard there that I hadn't seen before. It didn't feel right, considering she'd just sent a client spinning in discomfort. Despite the hand that was still resting on my shoulder, I thought she should have been softer still. The expression she wore was a guarded one, though, and I wondered what had changed in our time apart. *What do you think you know now?* I righted myself and grabbed the mug I'd originally turned for.

When I was facing away from her she said, 'I can't find Ruby Brinkley.'

I dropped a spoon with a clatter. *So that's it...*

Having never had children, I had no way of knowing how it was that parents coped with the harsh disappointment of being let down by someone you'd created. While I went back and forth, still, on my feelings towards Prue, in those moments I was driven by what I thought must be a maternal let-down; the realisation that having expressly told someone not to–

'I know what you said about not being able to find her...'

They'd stepped ahead and disobeyed you anyway.

Her excuses were a little like white noise while I tried to control my breathing.

'Yet,' I turned to face her when the exposition finally ended, 'you thought you'd ignore what I said about Ruby, what I explicitly said about the project in general, in fact, and do something about finding her anyway. Which you can't do. Like I said you wouldn't be able to.' There was spittle flying as I spoke and I knew I needed to control myself but the disappointment came in waves, like a river being dragged for a body. 'I realise your silence in this might be a stretch, as would be anyone's–'

'Erica, I don't think that's quite f–'

'Don't interrupt me, Prudence.'

She narrowed her eyes. 'Maybe I should go.'

I turned around to finish making tea. There was a teabag in her cup, too, but I didn't pour the water. 'Yes, maybe you should.' I listened carefully while I brewed my drink, in case she moved to leave, and then I took a seat at the table. I didn't look at her, though she stayed lingering in the doorway. In my peripheral vision I saw her glance at the sideboard, where her unbrewed tea was, and it crossed my mind that she might help herself to a drink; get comfortable; try to do another internal on an area I'd told her to leave well enough alone. If she was waiting for me to crack first, though, I knew she'd be sorely disappointed. Prue didn't know me well enough to know how I played my pawns in an argument.

While I was blowing my drink cool, she pulled out the chair opposite me and sat down. 'Why can't I find her?'

I threw my head back in irritation and spoke to the ceiling. 'Why are you looking?'

'She's important enough that you took her name.'

'It's a name no one is using!' I announced and I saw her interrogatory stare replaced with worry. I laughed; I couldn't help it. It was the hard-edged laugh that I could remember my own mother using too. Prue was making me wonder whether I'd missed my calling in being a bad parent to someone. 'Ruby Brinkley doesn't exist anymore.' I sipped my tea; the temptation to create dramatic effect was too much to resist.

She slapped a hand flat on the table. 'There must be more to that sentence.'

'Prue, make yourself a cup of tea and double-check your tone.' I gestured to the counter. 'Then we'll talk.'

'I don't think I want tea, Erica.'

There was a quiver in her voice and I thought, then, she must be terribly nervous – which was probably very sensible of her.

'There are newspapers in that chest that brand me as a handful from a young age. There's talk of me being rebellious. I think one even claimed that marrying Roger was an act of rebellion.' I let out a gentle laugh. 'What a boring rebellious act that must seem. Although the truth of it all is much different, which looks to be the theme of our time together, doesn't it? Because I didn't get myself in trouble, I didn't cause trouble from a young age. But I certainly spent time with others who did.'

She nodded along with me. 'Ruby?'

'Ruby was an excellent friend after Mum... Well, we'll come to Mum another day. Ruby was an excellent friend, though, and Dad adored her, too. During a dinner party once, he even went as far to joke about adopting her.' I stared hard into my tea to make a crystal ball of its surface reflection, as though the memory might form there. 'Her parents didn't say a word. Didn't laugh, didn't show mock outrage. I remember her mother flashing a tight smile and letting the comment slip by. That really hurt Ruby. She was spending more and more time out of the house after that. Sometimes she was here but sometimes she wasn't and, true to form, when she wasn't here and her parents called asking after her, Dad told me to plead ignorance; mind my own. I told him, once, that I should be providing her with an alibi, and he sat me down to explain why that was wrong. It's better to omit your knowledge of something, rather than lie about it.' I looked at Prue then. 'Isn't that a strange pearl of wisdom to pass on?'

She still looked wary. 'I suppose.'

'Anyway, after all that, even Dad was moved to help her in

the end. She'd brought trouble home one too many times and there was a fight,' I rubbed at my forehead to try to loosen the details from memory, 'it was one thing to bring the odd bit of trouble back, another to bring back a baby.' I sighed. Ruby had told me in confidence and I'd promised my secrecy until she told her parents. But when she'd arrived on our doorstep in tears, it had been harder to shield the issue from my own father. 'She told her parents she was in trouble, and that she wanted their help to source– to fund a termination. She'd decided it was the best thing.'

'But her parents?'

'Didn't want to fund it, also didn't want Ruby bringing a baby into the house. There was talk of marriage, making an honest woman of her; if only she'd say who the father was.' I sipped my tea and then searched for another memory in the ripples as I placed the mug down. 'Ruby was always loyal to a fault, regardless of her shortfalls.'

'So, you helped her?'

'Dad. Dad helped her. When she arrived in floods of tears one night, very late one night it was, she agreed to let me tell Dad what was happening. We both sat him down, as though preparing him for something that I'd done wrong rather than Ruby. In truth, I think he was quite relieved in that respect. But he said that he'd help her.'

'With a termination, this is?'

'With everything. Her parents had near as damn it thrown her out, but Ruby was near as damn it old enough to leave anyway. It would be a scandal when she'd gone, though, and she knew, Dad knew, they'd come looking for her.'

Prue's eyes brightened with realisation. 'You helped her to leave.'

'We helped her to leave.'

There was a long silence then, where neither of us felt

moved to offer anything more. I finished my tea and thought nearly a full minute must have rolled by before Prue finally spoke.

'I'm sorry.'

'For?'

She sighed. 'For looking for her. For not just asking.'

That was another technique borrowed from my mother. It was never enough to apologise; you always had to show her you understood your misdemeanour in full.

'Why don't you make the tea?' I pushed my cup toward her. 'I'll tell you more about Ruby, if you'd like. Although I don't want her mentioned in the book; I can't stress that enough. I'm happy to discuss my childhood, though, if you think it would be beneficial.'

'It would.' She flashed a tight smile. 'I want to make sure I'm getting your voice.'

'Very well. I'll breathe my secrets into a conch shell for you to hang on your laptop.'

She laughed. 'Are we writing a fairy tale ending?'

'I think my sunset is more likely to be the overhead lighting on a hospital ward.' She opened her mouth then, but before she had the chance to speak I pushed the mug a little closer again. 'But first, tea.'

She followed instructions, and my hostility towards her ebbed. But I couldn't say the same for Prue's own feelings. There was a tension in the hunch of her shoulders as she moved about the kitchen. She took regular pauses to cast an eye back on me and it stirred a worry; a nagging. *I wonder whether she believes me about Ruby...*

# CHAPTER EIGHT

I didn't lose my mother.

The house was silent when the yelp of my mobile cut through the air. It was a Sunday – Mothering Sunday, so said the kitchen calendar – and I couldn't think who'd be calling. In times like these the human brain tends to tread on the side of worry, I find: *I'd better answer; something must be wrong.* But I tried to resist the urge to let what would most likely be a telemarketer interrupt the solitude of a morning in the garden. A brood of ducklings had got into the bottom of my lawn, and I was set on watching them find their way out. The mother appeared occasionally, too, and I thought she must have found the exit-way but the children were unwilling – or perhaps even too frightened – to follow. When the mobile rang off I leaned my head back and closed my eyes, to sit in the warmth of the sun and only listen to the chirp of small critters. Until the godforsaken ringing started again.

'For Christ's sake.' I slammed my mug down with such a force that tea splashed over the rim. Then I hurried inside to catch the call before it slipped away. I was gearing up for an argument with whoever was on the other end of the line, until I came close enough to see the name. 'Prue?' She'd told me previously that she avoided work on a Sunday, and yet... 'This is a surprise. Is everything okay?'

'Have I disturbed you?'

*Yes.* 'No, no, everything is fine here. Are you–'

'Sorry, yes, I'm fine.' She sounded flustered. But truly, a woman of Prue's level of attractiveness couldn't be hard pushed for company, whether she was having a crisis or not, so I didn't know why I had ego enough to believe this young creature would call me – the accused and aged murderess – if she were in the throes of a panic. Then she asked, 'Are you busy today?'

I leaned forward to look through the window. The ducklings were watercolours, with the increased distance, but very much still there. 'No, I'm free the whole day. Did you want to meet for a talk about... well, something?'

There came a half-hearted attempt at a laugh then, and she said, 'You're sure you're free?'

'I'm more surprised you don't have better plans. Aren't you visiting your mother?' It was a fishing expedition. Prue had never said more to me about her family than the details she'd given when I first met her – that they'd been somehow misplaced.

Prue grew so silent then, that I thought the call had disconnected. But, 'No.'

I lingered for a minute in case there was more to come. But when nothing did I said, 'Righto. In which case why don't you pop over for a spot of Sunday dinner, say around two?' It felt like a brazen suggestion but still, she must have called with something in mind. And everyone needed to eat, whether they were in the middle of a disaster or not.

'You'll cook?'

I laughed. 'No. But I'll pay...'

We left our cars both on the driveway and walked the distance to the pub. I'd called ahead and heard from Hugh that it was a quieter day than usual, with the villagers' sons and daughters apparently stretching to something more glamorous than the local for dinner. But there was still a small carvery menu available, and Prue said that would be a welcome change from packet noodles. She tried to brush the remark off as a joke after she'd shared it, but it crossed my mind, then, that she might not be taking good enough care of herself.

On the walk down to Hugh's we hardly spoke. Prue looked around us like a cat who spied a sparrow; she was keen-eyed, twitchy. Every few breaths, she would take an especially deep one. I could hear a greedy pull of air and a slow push out. But apart from that she was hiding any panic well. Of course, she still hadn't said there was anything wrong. But I couldn't shake the feeling.

'Prue,' I started as we edged into the village, 'are you ready for curtains to twitch?'

She looked around us. 'I'm sorry?'

In my best overtly West Country accent I said, 'She's not from 'round 'ere.'

Prue burst into laughter and it was beautiful.

'Inside or out?' I nodded to the wooden benches.

'Will you be warm enough?'

*So you've noticed I need the warmth...* 'I don't see why not. What's your poison?' I looked at her in time to catch a wince. Her lips narrowed and her eye twitched like a knee-jerk reaction and I smiled. *Roger wasn't poisoned*, I wanted to say but I stifled the temptation, lest I ruin what could be a beautiful moment. 'Wine?'

'I'm driving, so I'll just have a lemonade.'

'I'll get a bottle, and a lemonade. You can always stay over.' I walked away before I could catch her reaction to my offer. But at the bar I wondered whether it had caused a second wince. If so, her face had fallen into neutrality by the time I was back with her. Prue looked around her with the air of someone unhurried, and I spotted another deep breath. I imagined her ribs expanding, lungs filling; the ease of it all. She smiled when she spotted me then, so I took a seat on the bench, opposite her so I could get a good look.

'Were you and your mother close?' she asked, when my rear had hardly touched the seat.

'I thought it was a non-work day.'

She laughed. 'Maybe I'm just making conversation?'

I took in a mouthful of wine and waited a second before swallowing. 'No.'

'Just no?'

'Just no.' Another sip. 'There are newspaper clippings in that trunk that describe me as motherless, which always felt very scathing to me; I don't quite know why. It felt as though it said something about *me* that I didn't have a mother to speak of, rather than saying something about her.' I took another sip then, and when Prue didn't fill the silence I carried on. 'In the very early days, people assumed she was dead. Friends, or rather new friends, people Dad met later in life. I think it's easier for people to assume that of a woman, isn't it, that she died on her children rather than abandoned them.'

'I think mothers are afforded a bit too much credit in that respect.'

'Mm, you're not wrong. The media made similar claims about Mum having died, too, until some clever dick thought to check death records and turned up with nothing. From then on I was motherless; childless. I worried midway through the investigations that someone might turn up on the doorstep one day and revoke my right to carry ovaries at all.'

Prue sprayed out her drink in laughter. 'God, I'm so sorry.'

I handed her a napkin. 'Don't be. It's nice to see you laugh.'

'You caught me off guard.' She dabbed at her mouth, composed herself, and then asked, 'Do you feel less womanly then?'

'For not having a mother?'

'For all of it, I suppose. For not having a mother, not having children; for everything that's been…' She hesitated. 'Well, everything that's been written and said over the years.'

It was a weighty question. Although she'd used her most relaxed tone to posit the query, I imagined there was a spring-loaded box sitting between us then. The slightest movement even, might be disturbance enough to cause all sorts of things to leap out. So I took my time in answering and punctuated my flurry of thoughts with one, two sips of wine.

'Not less woman,' I said in the end. 'Only a little less human.'

In a quick-fire motion she reached across to grab my hand and my knee-jerk response was to pull back – but I forced myself to stay in the moment with her. She ducked into my line of vision and pulled my stare up to her, to hook my attention, then she squeezed, released and rubbed the back of my hand. Her expression was soft and I imagined her blurred around the edges, so only her smiling face was in focus. It had been such a long time since someone had looked at me how Prue did then.

'Enough about mothers.' She pulled her hand away and, despite my initial reluctance, I wanted to reach after her. 'Tell me about your dad?'

'Ah, I don't think so. I believe you owe your own tale of motherly woe to this table.' I tried to use a jovial tone. But if she thought she was going to take feeling without giving something heartfelt in return she was mistaken.

She flashed me a tight smile and said, with a dramatic delivery, 'I, too, am motherless.' She set the back of her hand against her forehead and whimpered, as though she might faint from the admission. 'Childless, too, but the latter is very much by choice.'

'Your dad?' I pushed.

'Also not around.' She tapped my hand. 'Your dad.'

'Always around.'

'Ladies...' Hugh appeared with a plate of food balanced on each hand to cause an interlude in our telling. In truth, the interruption was a welcome one. There was a clot of feeling forming in the back of my throat like stomach bile that's risen and doesn't quite know where to go. While Hugh introduced himself with a full name and a handshake, I tried to swallow back the burn and replace it with the harsh vinegar of the wine that Prue still hadn't had any of. *And how will I get you to stay if you don't...* I considered topping up the spare glass while Hugh kept her occupied but it lacked the subtlety that I wanted. Besides, I didn't want to trick her into staying with me. I wanted her to choose it.

'Well, enjoy. You know where I am if you need me.'

'Thanks, Hugh.'

'Thank you.' Prue grabbed her cutlery. 'You were saying.'

'Only that Dad was always around.' The spring-loaded box that I'd been so wary of before suddenly burst. There were so many memories that belonged in a scrapbook; if only I hadn't spent time collecting newspaper clippings instead. Still, I could recall the most important things. 'He never missed a parents' evening; graduation; driver's test.' I laughed. 'Failed driver's test.'

'How many times?'

'Three,' I admitted begrudgingly.

'Snap!'

'He would always have me back out on the road the same day,' I remembered, with a warmth spreading through my chest that was equal parts feeling and alcohol. 'I would fail and he would ask on what and we would practise, practise, practise from the same day on. There was never a break. Not that he pushed me, you understand, only that– only that he never wanted me to give up on something because it was difficult, I suspect. He never wanted me to stop trying.'

'You must miss him a lot.'

'Every day.' I pushed food around my plate. 'It was the trial that finished him.'

'Yours?' she asked and I nodded. 'Do you mind me asking...'

'It's an understatement to say it was a stressful time, of course. But Dad gave it the same gusto that he gave everything else. He arranged my representation, never missed a court date, never missed a meeting with the police; even when he was forced to hover outside the room while they interrogated me for the hundredth time about whether my marriage was a happy one.' *Bastards*. My tone hardened. 'He had a heart attack six months after the trial ended. No one would ever say it, but it was the stress of it all, I know. He saw me set free, he got me settled and then he...'

'Erica,' she spoke my real name in a whisper, 'I'm sorry for what he went through.'

'Yes,' I straightened myself up, then, 'yes, so am I. But it can't be helped or changed. I was lucky that he was there for me how he was. Christ, even when he thought I'd killed a man.' Prue fidgeted in a way that put the smallest amount of extra distance between us, and I smiled. 'Apologies.'

Her forehead wrinkled. I imagined her going back and forth

on whatever it was she wanted to ask. 'Do you think he thought you did it?'

I leaned into the dramatic tension and took a sip of my drink before answering. 'At one time or another, I think everyone must have thought it.'

Prue gave me a nervous smile then, and dropped her eyes to her food.

*And even you're wondering, now…*

# CHAPTER NINE

I didn't plan to get pregnant.

Ruby and I had been close but we weren't *that* close. It was a coincidence more than anything, and she was long gone by the time it happened to me, too. The only true relief in it all was that I already knew how Dad would react; he'd had a test run with my best friend only three years earlier. I was two years into my degree when it happened and I came home, distraught, as though someone had told me the world might end any second. The man responsible – although he was more of a boy, really – shot me a wide-eyed look of pure terror when I told him, which I only did because the equalitarian in me couldn't abort a child without telling the father beforehand. But he was glad I'd made the decision on my own, I think; there was an observable relief in him, too, that I didn't want him to hold my hand on the way to the clinic.

'Do you want me to let you know when it's done?' I'd asked; common courtesy again.

He looked at me blankly for a second, then asked, 'Why?'

His father should have used a condom.

But then, so should I.

Prue pulled me back into the present. No longer Mothering Sunday; no further opportunities for me to be a mother, either. 'He didn't come forward during the trial?'

I shook my head and pulled my blanket closer to my chest. It was a painful day. 'No. I think kiss and tells only happen when it's someone you're proud to have bedded. Although I suppose he could have pitched a kiss and survived story that they would have liked, too.' Prue didn't say anything in response to that, though, she only went back to her note-making. We'd been talking for hours and I was exhausted but she seemed immersed in the narrative and I wasn't altogether ready to send her home. 'Ready?'

'Mhmm.' She drew a line under one portion of the page, as though ready to move on.

'I took a break from university for the year that it happened. I was midway through my second year already, so before the start of the second semester I applied for leave and it was granted without question. I think Dad must have pulled strings there, too, although he wouldn't admit to it. Anyway, a month later I was booked into a private clinic and it was all flushed out.' I half-laughed and felt a gust of wind shift through the rungs of my chest. 'Like a good deep clean, I remember thinking. Like they were scraping away all of the badness.' *Not that all rot can be dredged quite so easily.* Prue had finished her note-making, but she didn't look up. 'I'm sorry, is this too difficult?'

*Wait until we get to the murder accusations.*

She hesitated. 'I'm losing track on where this fits with Roger.'

'Oh.' *I'd almost forgotten.* 'I had my... procedure on January 23rd. I met Roger on March 1st. I'd barely stopped bleeding, although I was back to normal life. He swept right in and picked up the pieces of it all though.' I plucked free a loose thread on my blanket. 'Then he spent the first year of our relationship breaking other things.' When I looked up Prue was watching me, waiting for more. 'That's for another day.'

'Are you okay, Erica?'

'Of course.'

'You look a little... tired.'

I smiled and admitted, 'I am.'

'We can stop then?' She was already folding away her notebook and I wondered whether I'd given her an excuse she'd been desperate for.

'I like us talking.'

Prue tucked her book into her bag and retrieved her laptop in its place. 'So, I'll stay.' She looked at her watch. 'If you rest now, you'll be awake for dinner. I'll have typed up my notes. We don't have to talk about the book?'

'You'll stay just to talk?'

'Pff.' She was already tapping away. 'I'm staying to talk *and* eat.' She looked over the top of her laptop screen and winked, and the gesture sent a small ocean wave through my belly. 'I'll look at what deliveries are available in the countryside. You, rest. I'll be down here.'

I added 'guardian' to the list of things Prue was becoming to me.

---

The pain threw me awake. It ripped across my chest and left me gasping like a fish hooked, reeled in and discarded. Then it settled into stinging nettles; then, a dull throb. It was only an ache by the time Prue came to a stop in the doorway. For the entirety of my time in the cottage up to then, no one else had known the intimacy of my bedroom. Between that, and the jagged breathing from the lost hummingbird inside my ribcage, I felt uncomfortably exposed. I set a palm flat on my chest while my other hand worked through my hair; a tangled bird's nest, matted from restless sleep. I wondered how long I could pretend I didn't know she was there. It crossed my mind she might just leave.

'You're sick,' she said eventually. I was still staring at the ceiling. 'You want me to pretend I don't see it. But I've been able to hear it in you a few times now, and I heard it then...' She petered out. *Did she expect me to deny it?* Another few seconds rolled by before she asked, 'Should I go back downstairs and pretend I didn't hear anything?'

Roger had taught me to be autonomous in sickness. Although he hadn't minded the health and wealth aspects of the vows, whenever I'd been ill, though, I'd always been left in charge of seeing to it that I got better. Whenever he'd been ill, I became nurse then, too. But from the first time I was struck with a cold it became clear that I would buy my own Lemsip; tidy away my own tissues. We upheld that dynamic throughout our marriage, which had only made grieving his death that bit harder; I'd believed I could make him better, somehow, as though I could take back the fatal head wound.

After him, around the time my father got sick, too, I realised there was something wrong with me. The heavy breathing, the mucous; the inability to shift either, no matter the antibiotics. Dad had noticed I was unwell, intermittently, but even he'd become so accustomed to me getting better quietly – being sick quietly, too – that he'd only asked once or twice whether everything was okay. When I'd lied convincingly enough once or twice, he let the concern fade. It was the best thing for him, in truth; he'd had much bigger things to worry about.

Dad had already passed away by the time a doctor found the Sylvanian Family of tumours living in my lungs. I'd grown so independent in sickness by then, though, that I thought an oncologist's help would also be more of a hindrance.

'You refused treatment?' Prue set a steaming bowl of pasta on the table in front of me and I winced. She saw. 'I was struggling to get an internet signal, or a phone one for that matter, so I raided your cupboards. I'm sorry it's not...' She fizzled out and I heard the disappointment.

'Oh, it's not the food.' I rubbed at my forehead; there was a stirring of pain there, too, now I was upright. 'My medication can make me feel sick in the hours after I've taken it. Food can be,' I frowned at the bowl in front of me, 'challenging.'

'All food?'

I nodded. 'I'm afraid so.'

'In which case, it doesn't matter what you're eating.' She must have noticed that I'd moved my cutlery a fraction, because she pushed it back. 'I don't know much about modern medicine but if you're not meant to take a painkiller on an empty stomach then I'd wager you're probably not meant to take *your* painkillers on an empty stomach.'

'It wasn't a painkiller.'

'Which I think adds further weight to my argument if anything.' She tucked into her dinner, then, as though that was the discussion settled. But when I hesitated further she tried again to convince me. 'Erica, just a little?'

I laughed, and my hand flew to my chest to catch the pain. 'You aren't being paid to look after me.'

'No, this is just a bonus to the Prue Carr experience.'

*This isn't a safe experience,* I thought as I leaned back in my chair. 'I don't need to be–'

'Yep, looked after, I hear you. But we've worked all day and we haven't eaten, and we're both going to eat alone otherwise. So, why not eat now? Besides, you'll make me feel guilty if I'm eating without you.' She forked three pieces of pasta into one mouthful. 'And why would you do that?'

I only raised an eyebrow in response. She was endearing when she argued. The pasta was warm still, and piece by piece I made a concerted effort to work through half of the bowl. We ate with silence between us and the hum of music in the background.

'Thank you,' she said, when I admitted defeat. 'I know – well, I don't know. But I can only imagine this all can't be easy, and...' Again, she fizzled out. Her eyebrows pulled together in confusion and her posture stiffened. 'How long do you have?'

*Ah.* I sipped at the small measure of water I had left. *So she's realised why it's now...*

# CHAPTER TEN

I didn't keep up to speed with the release of new documentaries.

The rain had caught me off guard and, like half the village it seemed, I'd taken shelter in Edna and Bessie's cramped shop. There were small huddles forming, with the older women gravitating towards each other and the older men grunting and critiquing the British weathermen for having missed this downpour in their morning reports. I couldn't comfortably slip into either group: too female for one and too young for the other. Instead, I took up residence at a window and watched; there was a grey cloud hanging over the village. It reminded me of something from a science fiction programme I'd watched with Dad as a child.

'Penny for them?'

I was still looking out of the window when I answered. 'I'm not sure they're worth even that much.' It was Archie who'd asked; the only Cockney in the village, making him distinct from a mile away never mind when he was barking right next to your ear. I turned to flash a smile but my concentration slipped when I spotted what he was cradling: a small feline. She looked like a tumbled piece of tiger's eye. 'Out for a walk?'

He followed my eyeline down and laughed. 'She's an old girl now, doesn't get out much.' He took a cautious glance around the room. 'Mind you, I could be talking about any of them, couldn't I?' The cheekiness of the gesture reminded me of something my own father would have said, and I found that I was laughing along with him. When the humour settled, he nudged my elbow softly. 'You're looking very tired, Ruby, if you don't mind my saying so.'

This was one of my favourite sentiments passed around the village: 'If you don't mind my saying...' It was a privilege known by old and rude people alike. In my core I knew Archie was the former not latter, but still. There was an entitlement that whatever they wanted to say had *such* a weight of importance that it didn't quite matter whether you minded or not. The option of hearing was only afforded to you after the fact, though, and you just *knew* that more often than otherwise, it would be something you'd choose against hearing.

'Are you getting enough sleep?'

I hadn't been. But it didn't feel like Archie's business. 'It's old age kicking in.' I winked.

'Nonsense!' He seemed sincerely outraged; some people even turned to check he didn't need saving. 'You've got years ahead of you yet, girl.'

It would have hurt less, I think, if Archie had extended his old feline and let her tear ribbons of skin from my face. There was a prickling sensation in the corner of each eye, and I felt a flicker of sincere dislike for Archie, then, for having caused a quiet storm of sadness. Although he'd done it unknowingly, I reminded myself, and that was the important thing. People could get away with all sorts if they were only causing accidental damage.

'From your mouth to God's ears,' I answered, and looked back out to the rain. The grey of the cloud had deepened, but I was about ready to chance being washed away.

'You want to get yourself home when this knocks off, girl. Open something fancy, get something nice in the oven. Pop the telly on and get your feet up. Anything good on?'

'Good' might have been a stretch. But it turned out there was something...

A montage of Roger's face at different ages in his life flashed across the title screen. They conjoined to make a patchwork of something that I thought was meant to look like him at the age of his death. But in truth it was a poor attempt at being aesthetically edgy; one that made my husband the poster boy for a would-be murder mystery. The show was true crime according to the television guide, and from morbid curiosity I was drawn in on the wonder of how 'true' this latest addition to mine and Roger's canonical works would be. The production was unoriginally titled *Murder Unsolved: Roger Miller* – and I knew from years of experience that where Roger was mentioned, I likely wasn't far behind.

'Roger Miller came from a good family...' the narration started.

'Wrong,' I answered. I should have brought a notebook to bed with me, to keep a tally of inaccuracies.

'He led a quiet life, following in his father's footsteps of the family business.'

A curt laugh erupted from me, like water spilling from a broken tap, and the force of it scratched my throat. Roger's family had been trash can scrapings from a rough estate in the area. But he hid that well with practised Received Pronunciation and friends in high places. From a young age he was good at brown-nosing those who could – and would – help him to get whatever it was he wanted. Enough sweet-talking, and Roger could charm himself into or out of most situations – including a business meeting with my father, which was how he came blundering into our lives.

'When he was twenty-three he married his childhood sweetheart...'

There was a turn in my stomach, then, and while the narration continued I tried to block out the name that followed – because it wasn't mine. That was one of many stories that Prue and I hadn't come to yet, and it was one of the lesser-known details of Roger's life from before me. They often didn't include that on the documentaries, though, and despite myself I was impressed that this latest round of researchers had managed to upturn mention of The First Wife. I wondered whether they'd managed to find her...

Still, they scooted past a lot of the in-between information, landing heavily on the time when Roger and I first met instead.

I'd been travelling with friends along the coast while the weather allowed for it. It was my preferred way of skulking back to normal after the termination. But I'd come home when we all caught word of a storm that was teasing at the edges of England. I don't mind admitting that I was young and well-funded enough to think I could take off whenever I wanted, so it didn't bruise my plans to come home sooner. It did mean my father was booked head-to-toe with meetings, though, and that's how I met Roger. I waltzed into my home with damp hair, dragging a wheeled suitcase and a bunch of flowers that, as tradition dictated, I would give to my father and he would give back to me. It was something we'd done since I was a girl; I couldn't even place how it started.

'Bloody carnations if you can forgive me for it,' I announced as I fell through the front door, bringing a bang of thunder along with me. I struggled to drag my case over the threshold but my attention was caught by a voice that didn't belong there.

'No to carnations, then, duly noted.'

I looked up and immediately lost my grip on the case handle, creating another bang. 'Bugger.' It was a hard task but I pulled myself together and closed the door, then I took the man in again. He was beautiful – and my young heart thumped like a wild thing. 'Sorry, you are?'

'Roger.' He extended a hand. 'Roger Miller.'

'Erica.'

'A pleasure.' He straightened himself up, then, as though remembering why he was there. 'I've got a meeting– your father– he, ah...' He petered out and laughed at himself. 'Sorry, your father is in a meeting that's run over. I'm here to see him afterwards.'

I looked around. 'He left you loitering?'

'Ah, well, actually.' He pointed to the open doorway to the right of us, which led to the living room. 'He told me to make myself comfortable. I chose to loiter.'

'Do you want to loiter in the kitchen?' Heat pierced my cheeks as I asked, and I wondered what shade of red they'd shot to. 'You can even loiter with a tea or a coffee...'

He had smiled. His mouth was lopsided, a dimple one side but not the other–

There was a stabbing pain in my chest, then, and I didn't know whether it was the cancer or the memory. I imagined the growths as small angry creatures sometimes, kicking their feet out at not getting their own way. I pulled the duvet up to bunch it around my body for extra warmth. *No matter*, I reminded myself, *they'll get their way soon enough*, and I rested my eyes through an advertisement break.

A gavel landing with a thud against wood woke me. I couldn't remember drifting. But I'd slept through most of the murder and the subsequent investigations. As misfortune would have it, I'd woken up in time to see myself being hurried out of a court. They'd pulled good footage from somewhere; the panic on my face was painfully clear in high definition and I remember my solicitor – a close friend of Dad's – being a quiet support in my ear all the way to the car. When the door slammed shut on the vehicle I'd been hurried into, red and fractured block capitals appeared on the screen: NOT GUILTY. They hovered there for a second or two before being joined by a question mark.

'Bastards.'

'Erica Miller was found not guilty of her husband's murder. Although another suspect has never been isolated and, in the months after the trial verdict, the police were eventually forced to let Roger Miller's case slip into the cold cave of unsolved casework. Mrs Miller has been living off the grid since this happened, too, and if that doesn't cause suspicion then...'

'Miss,' I corrected them, and reached for my medication on the bedside table. When I turned back, they'd closed their sneaky mouths to let the credits roll. They'd picked the worst imaginable picture of me to end the programme, too. I hadn't slept when it was taken, after another long night of questioning, and my solicitor was again trying to fight us through the bodies outside of the station – the madding crowd that had been kept waiting. Someone saw an opportunity, though, and snapped, catching the bags beneath my eyes weighed heavy with the accusations that had been made. This had become one of many pictures to chase me around in the years since. Whoever had made the documentary had faded it out, to roll their end credits over the top of it. But the fade had somehow left my train tracks of mascara more visible. The police, I remembered, had worn me down that evening. After the seventh hour, I'd trod the line of confessing if only to finally escape the interview room. None of it was anything I wanted to remember yet there it was, waiting like a slim film of oil; always resting on the surface.

In the instant that the credits stopped rolling, my mobile chirped. It was late, so I assumed it was either a promotional offer or a mistake. That, or Colin had also watched the documentary and he wanted to make sure I wasn't hanging from a rafter. But when I glanced at the screen I saw Prue's name instead, and a message preview: "I know tomorrow isn't our day for it but..." The text had arrived in such synchronicity, I went to sleep wondering whether she'd watched, too.

# CHAPTER ELEVEN

I didn't know my husband was married.

When Prue arrived the following day there was something different about her. Her tone was curt, and she looked to be loaded with a list of questions that felt more informed than our previous talks had been. I offered to get out the next scrapbook in the series, but she asked whether it could wait a while; whether our talk might be more organic for the day. It seemed an odd ask, given that from my vantage point across the kitchen table I could see a list of bullet points on the paper in front of her. I nodded towards it.

'You don't look set for an organic discussion.'

She made a point of folding to a clean sheet. 'They were some thoughts I had last night.' She smiled, but it didn't look like her usual face, and for the second time since the credits had rolled I wondered whether she'd watched. 'Can we talk more about Roger?'

I poured tea. 'You don't mind working in a non-linear timeline?'

'I'm sure I can manage.' She rested her hand across the lip of her cup. 'I'm all dosed up on caffeine already.'

'I can get lemonade?' I started to get up.

'Erica, please.' She reached across the table and made a grab for my hand. 'Can we?'

I sat back down then and stared into the surface of my drink. There were small clots forming in the heat of the tea. The milk was turning. 'What would you like to know about him?'

'Did you...'

*Kill him?*

'Did you fall in love at first sight?' Her tone was softer. 'Did you know?'

I thought back to the unexpected coffee across my father's dining table and smiled. 'I knew something. I knew I liked his smile, which was always something I looked for. But I wasn't the settling down sort of girl, ever. So no, it didn't occur to me that I might be feeling early love, or something like it. Only... only early fixation.'

Her head tilted. 'That's an interesting word to use.'

'Hm.' I reconsidered but, *no, fixation is right.* 'I made Roger a conquest. I was quite driven like that, when it came to things I wanted.' I laughed and then corrected myself. 'People, sorry, not things.'

She smirked. 'How far can I push the personal questions?'

There was something of the old Prue about her then. Her facial expression relaxed into a thing I recognised from earlier talks, and her tone was jovial. Not for the first time, though, I felt myself pushed away from and pulled back towards her in a wave of feeling. I coughed to clear the seaweed from my lungs before I answered.

'I won't blush, but I'll certainly say if it's too far.'

Like a knee kicked from behind, her eyebrow arched. 'Did you sleep together early on?'

'I'd known him for a month.'

'That's a respectable amount of time,' she said, which I

thought made it sound like I'd been looking for her approval. 'I thought you might say you'd taken him there and then on the kitchen table.' She was noting something down as she spoke so I couldn't see her expression, but I heard the words crack partway through from a smile. When she lifted her head, though, she appeared neutral. 'You didn't want anything serious, I take it?'

'We're conditioned not to, aren't we?' I stood, then, without waiting for an answer and set the kettle to boil again. I couldn't do this without warmth in me.

'How so?'

'Women.' I turned to get a look at her reaction. 'Women are conditioned one way or another. Either to want a husband and babies before they've laid eyes on a man or, if they'd like to make themselves especially attractive to a male, then they have to pretend they don't want anything at all apart from his appendage.' The water started to boil in a percussion behind me. 'I think not wanting someone or even something is meant to make us more desirable, too, because men often want what they can't have, don't they? So, if you *don't* want to settle down, it becomes a greater challenge for any man if they can convince you to.' I didn't wait for an answer, only leaned forward to snatch my cup from the table and throw away the spoiled brew. 'Of course, all of that only works if you've got a man who thinks that way about "winning a woman over". Some men will sleep with a cold woman and think of her as just that. Cool.' I yanked open the fridge door and the chill hit my face with such ferocity that I knew I must be red, then, simmering. I grabbed a fresh milk and slammed the door. 'But there's always the chance in among all of this that you won't be a woman he even wants to win over.'

'And what happens then?' Prue asked quickly, as though nervous the chance to ask anything at all would otherwise slip by.

I turned and folded my arms. I couldn't tell whether she was altogether serious. A woman of Prue's age and intellect really ought to know. But perhaps her mother had never told her. I counted the options on my fingers. 'You're the woman who wants a husband and a child. You're the woman who wants neither, but he won you over and tamed you into it. And our third and final option,' my hands began to shake lightly, 'you're the slut.'

She looked as though I'd slapped her.

It took a while for me to steady, after I'd apologised profusely for the outburst. Although the apologies were interspersed with a refrain of, 'Still, I'm right.' So, Prue would have been well within her rights to doubt my sincerity. She was visibly shocked by what I'd said. But I refused to believe I'd told her anything she didn't already know. When I'd shuddered my way around the kitchen well enough to remake tea – and pour a tall glass of lemonade for my guest – I sat across the table from her and apologised again.

'Erica, there's really no need.' She grabbed her pen, then, and hurried to write something down, as though afraid she might forget a crucial detail. 'I don't think you're a...' She hesitated. 'You know, the word you used.'

It seemed a strange reassurance for her to offer, but still. 'Thank you.' I wondered at her reluctance to say the word out loud. *Did it cause general offence? Or am I not the first person to throw it at you?* When a woman hated a certain word, there was usually an underlying cause for it. I wondered, then, who might have called her such a thing. In the seconds after, she opened her mouth to add another detail but thought better of it, and instead wrote something else down. 'You look to be contending with a lot of introspection today.' When she looked up to me, I nodded at the notebook. 'Will it take an extra penny for your thoughts, or can I claim them as part of your initial fee?'

She looked uncomfortable as she answered. 'There are more things I'd like to know about Roger.'

'Well, I asked you not to do any research beyond the materials here–'

'No, I know but–'

'So you'd better start asking.' I didn't appreciate being interrupted. Still, I flashed a tight smile and she reciprocated. Something had grown between us, though, a tangible tension that became a centrepiece on the table. Prue looked troubled, too, her ordinarily pretty features pulled together to make a tight-knit frown as she browsed her notes. I thought of reaching across to cup the curve of her face. But it would take more energy than I could spare to bulldozer through whatever this growing unease was. I watched on and took two large gulps of tea while I waited. The drink was lukewarm now, which meant this holding pattern must have stretched on for longer than I'd realised. It spoke volumes, I thought, to how time must move when I was given the luxury of watching her work. But the wait felt dramatic after a while. 'Prudence.' Her head shot up at the sound of her full name. I wondered whether her mother had used it, too; whenever she was in trouble. 'This silence is costing me a considerable sum by the minute.' I'd noticed already, on a handful of occasions, how uncomfortable she became whenever money was mentioned. While there had been times, then, when I had so enjoyed her company that I'd forgotten her purpose for being there, I could only guess that Prue must have fostered similar feelings. The mention of billable time forced a half-laugh from her; a nervous sound.

'Okay.' She pulled in a deep breath. 'Did you know anything about Roger's past when you slept together for the first time, for instance?'

'You mean, how well did I know him?'

She hesitated. 'I suppose.'

The nerves came off her in small electric waves. But they seemed disproportionate for the weight of the clumsy question. But it all came together, then, a jigsaw in accelerated time-lapse to build a picture of an imagined Prue, perched on the edge of her seat – watching the documentary that had aired the night before. *So you did watch it; you do know about the old wife, the old life before...* I narrowed my eyes as though I might be able to find evidence of the film on her; flecks of (mis)information stuck to her clothing like lint. But of course no such evidence existed, and Prue's growing guilt was damning enough. Not everyone had a face that could carry guilt; life with Roger had taught me that.

'Roger was older by a handful of years. I had no illusions about him having been involved, or not, with women before me.' I paused to sip my cold tea and prolong Prue's observable discomfort. I wished for a word to describe what I imagined she might be feeling, but I couldn't settle on just one. 'It was no different to my having been involved with other men. Although the papers managed to resist making a meal of that.'

'You didn't have kiss and tells come forward?'

I laughed. 'It was in the media's interest to keep Roger's history out of the papers. If they wanted to capitalise on him being the prim and proper husband, it was always important that no one knew his bedpost had been whittled to a match.' I was beginning to sound bitter; I felt it. *Bitter enough to have killed my husband though?* I could see her trying to work out the answer to that. *But aren't all women bitter enough for it at one time or another?* I bit back on the temptation to ask her. She didn't have a spouse; she couldn't know.

'What about your bedpost?' she replied.

'What about it?'

'No one kissed, no one told?'

The cough-laugh erupted from me like water poured too

quickly down an old drain. It took me a second to catch my breath. 'Female murderers aren't sexy, Prue.'

Her eyes closed to slits. 'I'm sorry?'

'Charles Manson may have been a man of many wives,' I was careful to introduce this topic of marriage, 'but I can't recall men lining up for Myra Hindley. The conquests before Roger knew better than to lay claim to having escaped the clutches of a murderess.' I paused to wet my lips, then smiled. 'Accused, that is. Besides, in my experience men quite enjoy discarding a woman on the grounds of her being crazy, but they seldom never mean it. A jovial, clingy type of crazy may be an appropriate anecdote for over a pint. But a bludgeoned-her-husband-and-dumped-his-body is quite another.' I laughed, another eruption that made me wonder whether I was unknowingly nervous. 'No,' I reiterated, 'no kiss; no tell.'

Prue made notes in a hurry and I wondered what of this she thought would make it into the book. *Maybe she's planning her own...* But of course, we'd steered away from her real interest.

'Roger,' she spoke with her face angled toward her paper, 'did he only have fleeting relationships? There wasn't anything more substantial?'

*Oh, she's going to give me the opportunity to tell her myself.*

Her CV had mentioned journalism. I assumed it was that skill set at play now. Before I could answer, though, a sharp pain caught right in my chest and I rested my hand there, to let my fingers massage at the skin. It was a breakthrough pain, like light behind fractured pottery. I wondered how long we'd been dancing to this tune, for my medication to be wearing off. I realised, then, I'd need to stop the music soon and leave Prue waiting for the dregs of her answers.

'Roger was married when I met him,' I admitted.

Her face registered no surprise, not a flicker. Though she

wrote the information down, like it was something she didn't already know.

'Unfortunately, I didn't know that until I'd agreed to marry him.' I saw her scribbles pause. *They didn't tell you* that *in their little documentary, did they?* 'He made a stupid mistake when he was younger, and he married a woman who he couldn't afford to divorce. Neither of them had other partners to run off to, though, so they agreed to separate but stay married.' I tried to laugh but it emerged like a huff. I'd been so disappointed in him. 'He proposed to me before he'd even contacted her, just in case I happened to say no; he could have saved himself the struggle of tracking her down then.' There was an angry rush of rain that slapped against the kitchen window. It pulled my attention round and, quite without thinking, I said, 'Maybe I should have done.' I heard a sharp intake of breath from across the table. The rattle of the rain was distracting me from the spreading pains, unclenching like fists coming awake. 'When I said yes, he contacted her. But when she found out he was marrying into money, suddenly she had all these terms... Roger couldn't match what she was asking. So he went running to a grown-up for help.'

There was a long pause before Prue asked, 'That's when he came to you?'

I felt a tingle of tears as I shook my head. 'He went to Dad.'

# CHAPTER TWELVE

I didn't forgive my father for a long time.

Prue pushed for more answers but my stomach turned with leftover ill feelings. She could wait another day to finish her inquisition, I decided; even the Spaniards must have slept a day. And when she'd gone that's what I tried to do. But my mind was a tipped saltshaker and the grit of the memories kept me awake. Instead of staring into the ceiling for the third consecutive hour, I trod downstairs with a blanket around my shoulders. In the living room I lit the fire and left the room to heat, then I brewed herbal tea in the kitchen. There was a nagging chant in the back of my mind to watch my caffeine consumption. Although what my doctor thought that might do for cancer, I couldn't say.

There were certain things that, in recall, always felt mismatched. But I could still see Roger and his tired eyes and how he whimpered and– He was divorced in that memory though. *Was he married to me already when that whimper happened?* It had been the deceit of it all that left an unpleasant aftertaste, chased with the realisation that I couldn't trust my father anymore either. Although he'd redeemed himself when it came to the trial.

The kettle clicked and called me back into the room. I carried my drink into the warmth of next door and set it within reach of my seat. In the far corner, mostly hidden out of sight, there was an unmarked chest not dissimilar to the one Prue had been given access to. This one was full of scrapbooks, too: newspaper clippings; claim after claim; categorised by person, though, rather than newspaper. I pulled out the collection marked with a yellow sticker in the corner: Dad. Like a lonely child, I carried the book of bad bedtime stories back to my spot on the sofa, and read lies about my father to help me sleep.

The house phone jolted me awake. The heavy book fell and landed hard, and I rushed to answer the call. I didn't check the time. But I could feel things in my body that told me it was much later than I'd usually wake. I was missing the hit of painkillers – and the luxury of nicotine. I pushed a hand through tangles of hair that had encroached onto my face in the rush, and coughed a greeting into the phone. Sleep had strangled my voice.

'Mrs Miller?' a stranger asked. But I knew a doctor when I heard one.

'Speaking.'

'Hi there, I'm Dr Rowley and I'm part of the oncology team at Canon Heights General. I understand you've been waiting on some test results from us?'

I heard the turn of papers in the background.

'I know you've been dealing with Dr Knight throughout your treatment but I'm afraid she's on annual leave at the minute and she's asked that I–'

'How bad is it?'

I hadn't had a drink in hours or a smoke in a day, and there wasn't a seat in my hallway. So unless the good doctor was calling to say they'd found a cure for the incurable cancer, I couldn't afford for this to take so long. The alternative – the inevitable bad news, that is – meant I had even less time to spend on lengthy calls.

I heard her take a deep breath so I pushed. 'What's up, doc?' It was primarily to check she was still with me – in the moment. But also because humour is my best defence mechanism for these things, much to the disturbance of the doctors I'd dealt with.

'Mrs Miller–'

'Ms.' I shouldn't have interrupted her, really, after it had taken so long for her to talk at all. There was another audible breath, a near sigh that suggested she felt the same. So I added, 'My husband died several years ago...' to make her feel a little more awkward.

'The new medication,' she started, as though I hadn't spoken at all, 'it isn't working how we'd hoped. The tumours are growing at the same rate...'

She carried on, but I didn't hear much of what came after. I leaned hard against the wall and let my knees bend. There were lead weights forming in my stomach and I recognised the feeling from when another doctor had called; although the bad news had been Dad's, then, not mine. He hadn't been in good health for a long time by then. But when he'd been admitted to hospital that last time, it hadn't occurred to me that he mightn't make it out. I was in the middle of that memory when I realised the Reaper had stopped talking.

'I'm sorry,' I tried to tune back in, 'could you repeat that last part?'

'I only asked whether you have any questions? It's okay if questions come later though.'

I swallowed hard and realised then how dry my mouth was. 'How long?'

I imagined her flicking through stock responses. 'It's impossible to know for certain.'

There came a rustle of pain from inside my chest. I imagined one tumour elbowing another in glee. My knees cracked when I shifted and I realised, then, how close I'd sunk to the floor. If I were still married, Roger would be taking this phone call. He always dealt with the formal matters; I'd told him once that was what I paid him for. How would he handle news of me dying though? A sad laugh escaped. *He'd probably say it serves me right.*

'I assume it's safe to say, though, that whatever time we thought I had–,' the words caught in my throat, '–it seems fair to say I have *less* than that?'

'Yes,' she admitted slowly, as though she weren't entirely committed. 'But there's–'

'Dr Rowley, thank you for calling. I'm aware this is quite the baton to have picked up. I have to be going now, though, there are – well, there are things I need to be getting along with.'

*And apparently I don't have much time.*

When Prue arrived, she found me lunchtime drinking in the garden. I'd left the front door open and told her so in the voicemail I'd left, asking her to come over if she could make it – which I knew she would. Prue was hooked on the story now. I didn't harbour any blame, even, for her having watched the documentary. Any leftover fire in my belly for that had been replaced by the acidity of wine. Besides, if I were in her position then I'd likely have questions that I was too afraid to ask the accused killer as well. The scrapbooks full of things I didn't do couldn't answer to everything; they weren't designed to.

'Is everything okay?' She crept into my line of vision as though approaching something wild. But my expression was blank, still, from the shock of the call. 'Is this a working lunch thing or...' She tried to sound jovial as she nodded to the bottle.

'Working for you,' I answered. 'Liquid for me. Although I brought a spare glass in case you wanted to indulge. I'm glad you could make it over at all. I didn't interrupt plans?' I still didn't have a sense for how full her life was outside of this house. *Who would miss you?* I wondered as she sat opposite me.

She laughed. 'Typing up notes from yesterday were my plans.' She took care in positioning her face in a patch of shade. I thought she had a complexion that might freckle. 'There are things you wanted to add?' She was already reaching into her bag.

'A doctor called this morning.' I eyed the long stretch of garden ahead of us. When I first moved to the cottage, the thought of turning over the ground and sowing something new had kept me going. The large shrubs now looked full in this midday lighting and I felt a stab of envy for them. Prue was quiet for longer than I'd expected. I decided I'd give her until a still butterfly left the colour of nearby pansies and then I'd–

'Oh.'

When I turned, she was staring at the wine bottle.

'Oh indeed,' I answered, and she looked up. 'I'd like us to move a little quicker.'

'Still about Roger?'

'More about Dad.' I turned to face her fully. 'I want to talk about when the police came.'

Dad had near enough moved into mine and Roger's home by the time the search started. To begin with I'd assumed Roger had only left – in a huff, post-argument, which added to the evidence against me in the end – but it wouldn't have been the first time he'd disappeared like that. When money didn't disappear after him, though, I realised something was wrong. That's when I reported him missing. Dad said he'd wait with me for however long it all took; he was convinced, too, that Roger had only disappeared to spite me. Our conviction wavered as the days mounted and with every police visit – 'We're still searching, of course...' – our worries bloomed. My father had always been the type of man to throw money at a problem so he suggested hiring private firms, investigators, but I pleaded against that.

'Why?' Prue interrupted. I saw her glance at the wine bottle again.

'You're welcome to a small glass.'

'I'm driving.'

'It's a big house.' I looked away, and shook my head. 'It was all so surreal, I just– I wanted the police to do their jobs.' They *were* doing their jobs, of course. Even a team of private investigators wouldn't have been able to hurry the tide that eventually brought Roger home.

It didn't take long for me to become a side-eyed suspect either, though, which was another reason why I didn't want to antagonise the team whose help I depended on. They weren't aggressive or overt in their accusations, but there were certain questions that needed to be asked – 'And you say you argued?' – and I had to answer honestly because, well, at that time in the case I hadn't even entertained another option. But my father hadn't appreciated their tone – 'What are you accusing her of here?' – and he'd fought back the whole way.

Prue paused in her note-making. 'I'm sorry, can we back-pedal? Roger had left you?'

'Once or twice.' I topped up my wine glass. 'Will you have

some?'

She laughed. 'I'm getting to the point of needing it.' I knew she was joking but still I hovered. 'A small glass. I'm working.'

'And it's hard work, so a drink makes sense.' I poured until she said when. 'Roger had flings; we both did during the marriage. It's part of the reason why children never seemed all that important to either of us. Another thing that didn't make it into the papers.' I rolled my eyes and leaned back in my chair, and I tried not to watch how quickly Prue emptied half of her drink. 'Like I said, it only added to the evidence against me in the end, that we'd argued, I mean, that I had been the last person to see him; that I'd waited so long to report him missing, despite having good reason for it.'

'Your dad was your first line of defence, for explaining your reasons?'

I smiled. 'Always.'

He'd been steadfast in his support through to the bitter end. There wasn't a trial session he'd missed; not a second opinion he wouldn't pay for. They only had circumstantial evidence against me, but they thought it was enough – and it had been, when it came to getting me in front of a jury. But my father brought in everyone he could think of to dispute evidence. 'Of course there are trace fibres... Of course she waited to call... Of course... Of course...' They made everything sound so natural: the arguments; the evidence of my having touched his clothes, checked his bank, not even called his phone – on the assumption that I'd been abandoned, *again*.

I laughed. 'Dad was even my alibi for the night Roger went missing.'

Prue drained her drink, set the glass down and grabbed her pen. 'I think we missed that the first time around. He came over that night, too, after Roger left?'

'No.' I smiled. 'But he told the police he did.'

# CHAPTER THIRTEEN

I didn't have house guests often.

In a panic, I suspected, Prue quickly drank a second glass of wine after my announcement. But it wasn't until the alcohol collided with her empty stomach that she realised her error. She began to sway, even in the safe cradle of her chair, and each word came out knocking into its predecessor.

'You can stay here for the night,' I told her, and she'd been gracious about accepting the invitation. She was far too loose by then, though, not to look unnerved by the idea, as though she thought I might harm her in her sleep – which seemed quite a leap from a falsified alibi. I'd spent the rest of the afternoon explaining that I'd been alone the night Roger had gone missing. But my father – who had also been alone that night, later in the evening, at least – was savvy enough to know how it would be twisted against me if I couldn't account for my whereabouts. It likely would have come back to haunt him, too, had they ever sniffed around him as a suspect.

Prue worked hard to take notes and she tried to ask questions in the right places. But relief was tangible when I eventually suggested we take a break from work to make an early dinner. I'd told her to take a seat at the kitchen table, to keep me company while I cooked. I thought it might ease her worries to see transparency in my ingredients.

'This is the first time I've seen you look truly nervous,' I said, facing away from her.

There was a long pause before she answered. 'You just admitted to having lied to the police.'

'Now,' I turned with knife in hand, '*I didn't lie to the police, my–*'

'Semantics.'

I raised an eyebrow. 'Have you ever tried to talk a parent out of something?'

She laughed, and I wondered whether I'd managed to break the tension.

'You live alone,' I said, then, and she nodded as though it were a question. It wasn't, of course; I knew her living arrangements well enough. 'Imagine this, on any given night of the week, you're at home. How would you prove that to someone?'

She raised a finger and opened her mouth, like there was a quick answer to the question. But then she thought through whatever she'd been about to say, changed her mind and dropped her hand. She sank back against the chair beneath her. 'I... Well, I mean, there *must* be a way of doing that. I might have spoken to a friend, for instance.'

'And told them you were at home?'

'Yes.' She slowly shook her head then. 'Which proves nothing.'

Another raised eyebrow. 'Think on it. Perhaps while you're thinking you can pull a fresh bottle from the fridge. If you're staying, we may as well make the most of having each other's company.' There was a shuffle behind me, and I knew she was following instructions. It felt like a balance had been restored.

'We can talk shop over cooking, but I won't have it over dinner. If you've got topics for polite small talk up your sleeve, then I'd ready them now.'

She snorted. 'I think we'll be fine.'

Then I heard the splash of liquid hitting glass.

---

The morning after the night before, I left a pile of clean clothes outside of the spare bedroom that Prue had stumbled into. By the time the fire had burned down, and the third bottle of wine emptied, Prue had been worse off than I was. I'd even helped her to bed, one hand tucked beneath her armpit and my arm around her waist.

'This'll be the fluoxetine,' she said as we fell together through her bedroom door. It seemed an oddly specific choice to be a random one, although she laughed as though she'd been attempting a joke.

After I'd left the clothes outside of the door, I crept downstairs and set the kettle to boil. The house was as quiet as if no one else were in. I knew more about Prue, thanks to the loose tongue from the evening before, but I didn't know whether she was a late sleeper in the case of a hangover. Still, I readied two tea mugs and left hers without water. I'd showered, but for fear of waking her with the hairdryer I'd left everything damp, and in the hour that had passed my curls had started to form tighter than she'd seen them – and I wondered whether she'd prefer me like this. I tried to shake the thought away, and instead grabbed my cigarettes from the window and went to the garden, mug in hand.

The box rattled when I shook it, one stick knocking against another. Prue had smoked three last night – 'I'm not really a smoker.' – and I'd steadfastly refused her offers of, 'Just one drag?' The later it got the more she added to the persuasion: 'Come on, one won't kill you.' Her eyes had shot wide open in the aftermath of what she'd said, but I'd only laughed. Still, I refused the cigarettes – 'One a day, that's the rule.' – which made it more blissful when I sparked up and pulled in the first breath of it. I made myself a dragon, exhaled through my nose and ran a hand through my mess of hair. That's when I noticed the same two rabbits, from weeks ago now. *But how can you know if they're the same?* I wondered and smoked, wondered and–

'Doing it in your garden, too.' The sound of her voice made me jump. 'The indecency.'

Prue was wearing the jumper I'd left out for her, and a warmth spread through my stomach. I smiled and held out the cigarette box. 'Good for hangovers?' I saw a small retch form. 'Or not.' We shared a laugh but hers was tame, awkward. *Does she feel vulnerable in the harsh light of day?* 'There's water in the kettle, a teabag in the spare mug.' She nodded, and disappeared back into the kitchen without saying anything. *She didn't seem all that vulnerable last night...* I turned back to watch the rabbits again, but our morning greeting had scared them away.

The caffeine perked Prue up quickly in the thirty minutes after that, but she still seemed uncomfortable. She mustn't have spent the night with many strangers, I realised. Or perhaps not many strangers who have been tried for murder. I let out a little, 'Hm,' at the thought and she turned – 'Oh, nothing, sorry.' – then she quickly looked away again. We finished our teas in silence, waiting to see whether the rabbits might return. When they didn't, and I'd run dry, I suggested breakfast.

'Oh, you don't need to...' She petered out when she saw my expression.

'Don't worry, I won't.' I stood and held out a hand to her. 'Hugh does an excellent cooked breakfast, though, and you were far too tipsy last night for it to be safe to drive this morning.' She eyed my hand, then stood without taking it. But still, she smiled. 'Besides, the walk into the village will do you the world of good.'

She agreed to it all with small non-committal sounds. But the fact that she pulled her hair into a clip and shrugged her jacket on showed me she at least knew I was right – even if she didn't want me to be. Prue hovered at the end of the driveway, then, while I locked up.

'I'm sorry about last night,' she said, when we were walking.

I stole a quick look at her. 'Is there vomit in my spare room?'

She laughed, then answered, 'No, I just mean–'

'Don't. It was the most fun I've had in a long time.' I was being sincere when I said it, too. I couldn't remember the last evening I'd spent drinking wine in good company. Even if it was company I'd paid for. I let out a little huff of laughter, then, as something occurred to me: *This must have been how Roger felt with his women.* I made a show of checking my watch. 'You can be back on the clock now, if there are things you want to ask between now and when my black pudding hits the table.'

She made a clucking noise. 'Black pudding?'

'I'm not paying you to judge me,' I joked. But it sometimes felt like I was.

Prue didn't say anything for what felt like a full minute or so. She only looked around us, surveyed each field as we walked by it. The village was still a distance away, but certainly within our sights, when she said, 'Does anyone else know your dad lied?'

'Everyone,' I answered plainly. But I soon corrected myself. 'Sorry, everyone suspected he'd lied. No one knew for certain because – well, the men in my life were always good at covering their tracks, let's put it that way. In court they asked whether he was with me, and when he said yes, they introduced evidence to suggest he wasn't.'

'What was the evidence?'

'A credit card transaction from the night Roger went missing. For a steakhouse.'

'He was having dinner with someone?'

'His credit card was stolen.' I smiled, and I knew Prue caught it. 'He hadn't had the chance to report it, of course. In fact, he hadn't realised it had gone until some days later. He's a busy man, firstly. He had more than one credit card, ergo, he was always less likely to notice when one went missing. And he was comforting me for most of the days between that dinner and when he *finally* realised the card had gone.'

'There weren't cameras in the restaurant?'

I smiled again. 'Apparently there were. But they hadn't been working.'

Prue stopped at that, and I came to a halt a couple of steps ahead of her. 'Wow.'

I couldn't decide whether it was disbelief or judgement. 'What?'

'Is there anyone your dad *didn't* have in his pocket?'

I laughed. 'I'm afraid we'll never know.'

'Erica, did...'

I saw that flicker of wonder in her then. *Go on, ask.* I was desperate for her to.

'Did you never feel bad?' she asked instead and, disappointed, I picked up my walk.

'Not bad enough to go to prison for a permanent residency if that's what you're asking. The time I spent there throughout the case and the trial was quite enough.'

She took another big breath as though steadying herself. 'Was that the only evidence?'

'Against Dad? Not quite. They'd got my call records, so they knew that I'd called him, and they knew that I'd called *after* Roger left because of the timeline I'd already given them. All that really proved, though, was that a woman had an argument with her husband and called her father for an ear. He came over when he heard my upset, and he stayed.' We were nearing the village. 'Come on, come on, the timer is on you now.' I tried to joke but her nervous laugh told me it hadn't quite landed.

'What evidence did they have against you?' I made a noise and she added, 'It's a fair question and one that I'm going to need to know the answer to.'

'Roger slept with other women; Roger slept with prostitutes; I was an unhappy housewife. My alibi was shaky. I hadn't called Roger's phone, at all, in the days after he'd left.' I knew it was all coming out disjointed, non-linear. But I hurried to remember as much as I could in the time we had left. 'Oh,' I clicked my fingers, 'the browser history on my laptop showed that I'd looked up coastal destinations and–'

'Sorry,' she nearly laughed, 'why did that matter?'

'Because of where he was dumped,' I answered plainly, and the words landed on Prue with a blunt force. She must have known already, of course, from the documentary she lied by omission about. But I suppose it's one thing to know, and another thing to hear from the mouth of the woman you just spent a night with (sort of). 'I hasten to add, that's *not* why I was looking at coastal getaways. I went away alone sometimes; sometimes I went away with Roger. I was idly browsing destinations two days before we rowed. See,' I made a whoosh sound, 'the evidence goes away, just like that.'

Another nervous laugh. 'What else?'

'Prue, you aren't writing anything down. Isn't this a waste?'

'I've a feeling I'll remember.'

*Well, that seems fair.* I nodded then, and said, 'I suppose it's difficult, working with me.'

And the comment seemed to genuinely shock her. 'Erica, no! I... God, have I...'

'You haven't given me that impression, no.' I filled in the blank. 'But I can be a little...' I stuck out my tongue to one side, crossed my eyes and swirled my finger in tight circles. She snorted with laughter, and the sound soothed me. 'Speaking of which, can I ask my own question? Now we're spitting distance from a cooked breakfast.'

'Christ,' she said in surprise. Her tone had relaxed to friendly. 'I am genuinely hungry.'

'Brilliant.' I stopped and waited for her to as well. When she faced me I said, 'My turn?' She agreed. 'Now you know so much about me, why don't you tell me why it is you're taking fluoxetine?'

## CHAPTER FOURTEEN

I didn't know how much information she'd find.

Digital footprints made it far too easy to find out anything these days. Or so I was given to believe by those in the know. I didn't consider myself old, or even close to it, until someone talked me through algorithms and– other words that slipped my mind as soon as I'd heard the definitions of them. But, no matter the means and methods behind all this tracking, I was uncomfortably aware that Big Brother/Sister/Uncle was watching us. It had made it difficult to disappear, although money had certainly helped. Money had been a saviour a handful of times since then, too, and it left me wondering how anyone *without* money ever managed to hide anything – or track anyone down.

It was so bright that I had to wear sunglasses to drive, even though the temperature was base enough to leave me in a thick cardigan. *I should have brought a coat*, I thought as I climbed out of the car and another chill hit me. It had been such a long time since I'd driven into the guts of the city. I'd flirted with the outskirts for essential visits. But it may well have been the first time this car of mine was meeting a multi-storey car park, with its thick concrete and echoes. I coughed in the face of the wind, caught my chest before the pain could rupture it, and hurried toward the lift. Although the whiff of urine and leftover cigarettes had me rushing for the stairs soon after. *Not that the cigarettes are so bad.* Still, everything about the building said Big City, and it had been a long while since I'd felt comfortable in one of those. When I burst out onto the street I felt grateful for the hit of fresh air, even though there was construction noise carried along it, with a background percussion of car horns and hollers. *Everyone here knows everyone here,* I thought as I hurried through a conversation that was taking place over two lanes of stock-still cars, *and the traffic jams are as bad as they always were.*

Before now we'd only met in the office. But at her request we were meeting elsewhere today; it wasn't my business to know why. Although as I ducked down one street then another, swerving bicycle messengers and hassled businessmen every few feet, I thought she could have at least picked somewhere closer to where I'd abandoned my car. The longer I walked, though, the better a rhythm I got into. After the third shout of, 'Excuse me, please, I'm in a hurry,' from somewhere behind me, it dawned on me what the attraction might be to existing in a place like this: *Who even* knows *you exist here?* In the years since Roger I'd had to work hard to be anonymous. But now here anonymity was, being served to me in a business dealing out in the wide open.

The coffee shop, which was tucked away underneath a set of old train-track archways, looked suitably discreet though, and the corner that I eventually found her stashed in only added to the secrecy. I wasn't sure why she felt the need to be so cloak and dagger. Although it crossed my mind that she might be ashamed of her client. But I quickly laughed the thought away as a product of ego. She must have dealt with people bigger and badder than me before.

When I came to a stop opposite her, she glanced up from her laptop. 'I started a tab.'

'Are you...'

She waved away the end of my question and went back to her typing. I ordered a pot of herbal tea. I'd been awake for hours anticipating this meeting and the last thing I needed for the drive home was tired adrenaline rushing through me. They said they'd bring the drink over so I trod back, took a seat and waited for her to notice me. I didn't like being on this side of a business dealing; something about it didn't taste right. The discomfort only worsened when she raised an index finger, I assumed to signal my wait time, so I glanced around the room and counted quietly until she finished.

'Sorry,' she eventually said, and I was glad she'd had the decency for that. 'Work.'

'Yes, well.' I reached into my handbag and pulled out a light-brown envelope. It landed on the table between us with a thud even though I didn't drop it from much of a height. Still, I saw her smile at the noise. I wondered whether she could verify the sum from the sound alone. 'It's all there, present and accounted for. You can...'

She held up a finger again. 'I trust you, Ruby.' She leaned hard on my not-name and I couldn't help but feel like she didn't really trust me at all. Still, she only pulled the envelope toward her and tucked it out of sight in her laptop bag. Then replaced my monetary offering with an A4 folder. 'There's a lot here. Do you want the highlights?'

'Please.'

'Peppermint tea?' A waiter interrupted us.

'Hers,' she answered quickly, as though not wanting to be affiliated with the drink. When he set the cup and saucer down, she was quick to pick up with her thoughts. 'Well, Prudence Carr has led quite a colourful life...'

Terry Hetherington was an old friend of Colin's. Although given the age difference between them, I couldn't quite see how that added up. Still, she was efficient, discreet and, as I was fast to learn, bloody good at her job. Colin implied that he'd used her with other clients, although he'd never be brash enough to outright admit such a thing. But as she laid out the intimate details of Prue's past, I could see how having someone like Terry on the books – or not, as the case may have been – would have been helpful. If I'd known her when Roger was alive, things might have worked out very differently. I coughed a laugh. *Were you even born when Roger was alive?*

'Still with me?' she asked.

'How old are you?'

'Why?' She raised her eyebrow. 'Wondering how I'm so good at this?'

'Something like that.' I sipped my tea. 'What else do you know about Prue?'

'I know she has aspirations to be a novelist.' She handed over a sheaf of papers for me to skim through. 'That's just a Greatest Hits of the rejection slips she's received from various publishing companies for different manuscripts over the years.' It didn't seem newsworthy that she was a failed fiction writer, I thought as I skimmed the Thanks-But-No-Thanks letters. After all, weren't most authors? 'She started ghost-writing for quick and easy money when her debts started to pile up.'

'What debt?' I took another sheet of paper from her and stretched my eyes at the figures.

'Ghost-writing pays well, it turns out, and she'd need it to, to clear the sums. But it's been around three years now since these figures stopped going down at all. She's just about staying afloat finance-wise. As for where the money is going,' she held her palms up, 'you're going to have to leave that with me.'

'Do you have suspicions?'

She clicked her fingers to get the attention of a nearby waiter. 'Can I get a sandwich?'

'Your usual?' he asked, and she nodded before shifting her focus back on me. I wondered how many business meetings she must hold here on the average week, for them to know her sandwich order. I wondered, too, what her first job must have been as a teenager – because there's no way she'd treat a waiter like that if she'd ever been one.

'Gambling seems most likely. These days it's the easiest to hide, with so much of the legwork happening online. But it isn't very...' She fumbled about for the right word. 'Female.'

I raised an eyebrow. 'I'm sorry?'

'Women drink. Men gamble.'

'Is that statistically accurate?'

She smiled. 'I'm just speaking as I find.'

*I don't know about that. I've taken my share of risks.* I sipped my drink to stop the thought escaping.

'Do you know who she's close to?' I asked.

'Tight-knit circle of friends. It looks as though a lot of them met at university and never drifted away. There are quite a few in the same or similar industries, too, so there's an overlap between colleagues and friendship groups.' She was reading from a sheet in front of her. It crossed my mind that she could have emailed these details and saved me the inner-city stench. 'She's part of some writers' groups, so she attends fairly regular events for that.'

'How regular?'

'Twice monthly.'

*So someone* would *miss her.* 'What loose ends are there?'

She slipped the sheet of paper into a larger folder then, and handed the information over. 'You're in a rush?' The waiter set her sandwich down and she afforded him a thank you, which eased my desire to be rid of her company a little. There was hardly a beat of hesitation before she picked up what looked to be a grilled cheese sandwich and took a sizeable bite out of one edge. I don't know what expression I made, but she immediately apologised and half-laughed. 'I haven't eaten all day.'

I set a hand flat on my stomach. *Had I?*

She held the sandwich out. 'You're welcome to a bite?' I shook my head and she retreated at a speed; she looked glad of my answer. 'Prue also likes grilled cheese sandwiches. Her favourite colour is orange, like, bright burnt orange. Her favourite book is *The Velveteen Rabbit.* Her mother and stepfather are deceased and her half-sister lives near-on 400 miles away although they look to talk fairly often through–'

'Rewind,' I paused her. 'Half-sister?'

'Connie.' She took another mouthful and spoke around the bread. 'Married to Bertie, short for Robert, haven't worked out what Connie is short for yet.' In the pause for air she also dabbed grease away from the corner of her mouth. 'They have two kids but it's been hard finding the names for them. They're pretty careful of social media in that respect. But public records should come through for that.'

Prue had told me she'd misplaced her family. Her lie rang in my ears. 'Father?' Terry shook her head. 'He's also deceased?'

'Unlisted. Her mother registered as a solo parent. Father unknown. Different dad to Connie, though, whoever he is.'

I took the folder from the table and rested it in my lap. There was an anxious pain spreading in my chest and I needed to leave, but something tugged at me still. 'Is there any evidence to suggest that she's tried to find her father?'

Again, Terry shook her head. Her mouth was full of toasted crust but she waited until she'd swallowed this time to answer. 'None whatsoever. There's also nothing I can find to suggest her mother got child support of any kind from any mystery donors. Prue and her mother were on their own until Sid – Connie's dad – came along. No signs of animosity between Sid and Prue though. He's in all of her graduation photos, smiling like a doting dad all the same.'

*Which means nothing.* 'Thank you, for all of this.' I pushed my seat back. 'I'm sorry, I'm a little under the weather, I think, I should– let me get your tab, too, won't you? I'll settle up on my way out, if there's nothing...' I fumbled for words as I fumbled, too, for my bag. The cardboard folder was too big for the tote I'd brought with me so instead I held it against myself like a chest plate of armour.

Terry wiped her hands clean as she swallowed another mouthful. 'Look, ah... Ruby?' My eyes narrowed at her tone, and she held a hand up in a defensive gesture. 'Hey, it's none of my business. I'm not paid to care who you are. Colin vouched for you and,' she tapped the table where I'd set the cash down earlier, 'you pay your bills. So, we're on good terms.'

'Okay.' I pulled in a greedy breath. 'Okay, so, there's more?'

'I don't know what this Prue woman is meant to know about you.' Terry paused as though waiting for an explanation, but when I didn't give her one she turned towards her bag. She pulled out an A4 sheet that was creased around the edges. 'But whatever she's meant to know,' she handed the paper over as she spoke, 'I'd wager she knows a helluva lot more...'

`Recent search history:`

- Erica Roger Miller trial
- Roger Miller suspects
- Roger Miller cold case
- Erica Miller found not guilty
- Erica Miller murderer

# CHAPTER FIFTEEN

I didn't know how much everyone would love a monster.

The living room was a mess of lies by the time morning rolled around to meet me. It hadn't registered until then how late it was – or rather, how early. I pushed myself up from the floor and left the strewn papers behind. She was due to arrive in an hour and I'd decided by then that I'd let her have everything. If Prue was so desperate to know the truth, it felt right to accelerate the process and serve it to her; maybe then she'd stop looking.

In the time that I had left ahead of her arrival I took myself upstairs to shower. I managed a five-minute lie-down afterwards, too, before the weight of my thoughts became too dense, and then I carried on getting ready. My hair was wet and my eyes looked tired and my jumper was two sizes too big – another change since treatment had started – but I reasoned that if I was going to live through the mess of Roger, I may as well be comfortable for it. When I was downstairs again I brewed tea and took my single cigarette from the packet to enjoy in peace. I registered some hunger, then, or sickness that could have been hunger. But I didn't want her to catch me in the intimacy of breakfast. Whatever pangs I was having could wait until she left.

The smoke hit the back of my throat and my chest tightened with each inhale. Still, it was worth it. Everyone needs a vice, and I'd already given up so many of mine. When I squashed the butt in the outdoor ashtray, the front door bell chirped. But my watch showed another ten minutes before she was due. It wasn't like her to be early, although this was the first appointment with her since my meeting with Terry a week before.

It had been easy to let Prue down, with reminders of how sick I was: '*Cough.* Just so unwell at the minute. *Cough.*' Plus I was the one controlling the purse strings; another fact I readily reminded her of. But two days ago I'd bitten the bullet and called her, to arrange for this, today. From kitchen to porchway, it crossed my mind she'd arrived early in case I'd been planning a last-minute phone call to back out – which I'll admit had crossed my mind. Still, when I opened the front door to find Prue, a lost lamb looking about her green surroundings as though she'd never seen the place before, I was glad I'd seen our plans through. *Now to see through with the rest of it...*

'You're early.'

She checked her watch. 'Shit. I can wait in the car?'

From her flash of panic, I thought it was a serious suggestion, too. 'Don't be ridiculous.' I stepped aside. 'Come in, make yourself at home. Go straight into the kitchen, though, will you? The living room is a crime scene.'

I saw a flicker of something in her face, but she only smiled in response then ducked across the threshold. She followed the hallway along to the kitchen, like she had so many times before. And she had no idea what was coming...

The scratch of her pen against paper was the only noise for nearly a full minute. In my peripheral vision I saw her look up and catch me gazing into the garden, and I assumed she didn't want to interrupt my momentary break. We'd been talking for nearly an hour with little gaps between the narrative. I felt so time-pressured to get everything out in a rush. It worried me that I might become an angry tide, one that might lose momentum before escaping the sea wall; I needed to keep my gusto. I pulled in and pushed out air, then reached to open the kitchen window a little wider before I turned back to her.

'Where were we?' *I knew the answer. But I wasn't ready for what was coming next.*

'Roger's affairs, one mistress having got in touch...'

I half-laughed. 'That was it. She obviously thought I didn't know. I don't know whether she expected to ruin a marriage or... Well, I really don't know. But she had a price just like the rest of them. I can't remember how much it took but it wasn't anything extortionate, really.' Another near laugh. 'Despite what Roger thought of himself, he wasn't worth much to any of them. Which is fair, I suppose, given they were never worth much of a sum to him.'

'How did you keep all of this hidden?' She gestured at the growing list of details. 'All of the women, where were they during the trial?'

'Prue,' I was disappointed in her, 'you've seen your own non-disclosure agreement.'

She narrowed her eyes. '*None* of them could talk?'

'People always crack for the right sum, unless you gag them for a better one. Tea?'

The tag-on threw her. 'No, I don't– no, thank you. Erica.' I was facing away from her by then. 'What if one of these women had something to do with Roger's death?'

'They didn't.' I snapped it with too much certainty, and I

was glad she couldn't see my face. Although it crossed my mind that she might have only asked the question to get a reaction. 'Those women are just more entries on the lists of things that did, didn't, did, didn't happen.' I tried to keep my tone light while I filled the kettle, fetched the milk, busied myself. 'By the time Roger went missing it had been nearly a year since he'd had an affair.'

'Do you know why?'

I turned and shrugged. 'He and I were closer, I suppose. He mightn't have felt the need anymore. Of course, we were more like friends than we were anything else by then. But I think that happens to most married couples. I didn't push him away, especially. Nor did I pay for an alibi, stage my innocence, or buy the best legal team that money at the time could afford.' I joined her back at the table while I continued to rattle off the list. Every now and then she would write an entry down, something I hadn't admitted to before, I guessed. 'I didn't become estranged from my father during or after the trial, I didn't call on friends in high places, nor did I,' I couldn't keep my face straight, 'seduce the jury.'

'It's not laughable,' Prue answered. 'Women have done all those things before.'

'Ah, well in that case perhaps I was riding on the coat-tails of the murderesses who went before me. That'll explain the sensationalist literature that's sitting in the living room.' I sipped my drink and tried to steady the rising irritation. 'Perhaps I should scrap the memoir entirely and make a collage novel as a homage to Wilkie Collins.'

She stopped writing. 'Why aren't we working in the living room?'

'I had a walk down memory lane,' I answered plainly. 'The scrapbooks are all over the place and I'm happy for you to have a look at them, because they're better than any research you'll be able to do on the godforsaken internet.' She opened her mouth to deny the implication so I rushed to add, 'If I were you, I wouldn't make the mistake of insulting my intelligence with the lie you're about to tell.' There was a flash of something – panic, or even suspicion – and she leaned back slightly, then, as though putting further distance between us. 'All I want is the chance to tell my side of the story.' My throat was full of feeling by then, and it cracked across my words. 'That's all any woman ever wants. And I'd wanted to do it in my own time but,' I sighed, 'apparently that's too much of an ask as well.' It was a pointed comment but I couldn't work out whether it was the mass of tumours or Prue's secret research that was hurrying me. From the sad face she made, I thought she might be wondering the same.

'I'm sorry if I've hurried you.' She sounded like a caught child, and I felt like a scorned parent. I could only bring myself to sigh again, then, and I rubbed around my temples where there was a building ache. 'You're the project manager here, and the client, you're allowed to set the pace that we move at.'

*Except I'm not,* I thought, *and I can't.* 'There are things you want to know.'

'Need to know, for the sake of the project.'

I shook my head. 'No, Prudence, there are things you *want*, not need.'

There was a long and overstuffed pause, then, where she held eye contact with me. Before then, I wouldn't have thought she had such a look of confrontation in her. But I sensed she knew we'd come to a breaking point. When the silence became too much, though, I said, 'Ask.'

'Where were you the night Roger went missing?'

My head gave a sharp twitch; it was an involuntary response to an unexpected question. *Why would it be that of all things you want to know?* I narrowed my eyes, inspected the query for lameness or trickery. The only explanation I could find was that whatever she thought I was capable of, murder mustn't have been high on the list. I thinned my lips and thought hard about how to phrase my answer. 'Are you asking for the book or for yourself?'

'The latter, mostly. The former will be your decision to make.'

I was glad of that, at least. It felt like a safety net, sturdy enough for me to admit aloud for the first time that, 'I was with a prostitute by the name of Marcus.' I rolled my eyes. 'Sorry, I think sex worker is the preferred term. In truth, though, with the graft they put into their work they deserve a name of their choosing. So, we'll say sex worker. He and I had been seeing each other for two years fairly regularly. Sometimes we had sex, sometimes we talked, sometimes we sat quietly and kept each other company. I paid him a handsome sum for the privilege of our time together and Dad paid him a handsome sum to keep his mouth shut.'

'Your dad knew?'

I let out a huff. 'Prue, my father knew everything.'

'Did Roger?'

'Roger knew there were other men. I don't know he knew the... arrangements I had.'

'You wanted to keep it away from the press?'

'Christ, of course I did,' I snapped. I felt a heat in my cheeks. 'You've seen the things they printed about me *without* any evidence for half of it. Can you imagine the scandal if they'd have known the company I kept?'

'Where is he now?'

It seemed a strange question. 'I've no idea.' I saw her eyebrows pull together in worry and it clicked then. 'You want to check out my alibi.'

'It's not that. I–'

'I never knew his real surname,' I interrupted her. 'So I can't help there. But if you're desperate then I can tell you my father bankrolled a degree in business management at Bournemouth University. You could always beachcomb your way through admissions, if you've got enough free time to play detective.'

'I didn't mean... I'm sorry, Erica.'

'For?'

She sighed. 'For pushing? For asking questions?'

'It's the journalist in you, isn't it? Your kind are always sniffing out a story. So, here it is,' I leaned forward to close the gap between us, 'Roger and I argued the night he went missing. He wanted to buy more property, play house somewhere down on the coast, renovate something that I would have the privilege of paying for. It was another hare-brained plan that he'd bore of halfway through so I said no, we shouldn't, I wouldn't, what have you. He called me cruel and controlling and... hideous other things that a husband should never say to a wife, especially one that's paid for him ten times over. He left, and I was livid, so I called Marcus. He came to the house. We – what have you, and he went home. I called my father to be angry that Roger wasn't back yet.' I leaned behind me to open a kitchen drawer, and I pulled out an old Nokia handset. 'And that's the phone I called Marcus from beforehand.'

Prue stared, her eyes only slits now.

'It's the phone I used to arrange meetings with him, and one or two others over the years. See, unlike my husband, I knew how to keep more than just myself happy. I didn't boast about my affairs; I didn't sleep with homewreckers; I didn't shit where I ate.'

The heat that had before spread through my cheeks was now running through my whole body. Down to my fingers felt warmer than usual, and I could imagine the red patch of rage that had spread across my chest. It was hard – harder than usual – to take steady breaths.

'Erica, are you...' She reached across the table to grab my hand. 'Are you okay?'

I shook my head. 'That isn't what you want to ask.' I took another jagged inhale. 'Ask.'

Her breathing looked laboured, too, then, as she pulled in a greedy mouthful. I had a sudden flash of her drowning. 'You didn't kill your husband.' Her eyes were closed when she said it. I couldn't overlook the phrasing; the fact she still hadn't quite asked. When I didn't respond, though, she said again, 'And you didn't kill your husband?'

I smiled then, and thought: *At last...*

# II

## PRUE

# CHAPTER SIXTEEN

What's the word for when you're starstruck, but in a this-person-murdered-their-spouse kind of way?

Rita had been bending my ear down the phone for nearly an hour about the latest job she didn't want to do. She was a photographer at a modelling agency; a post she hated passionately. But Rita, like most people tied to the arts, realised she was lucky to have a job at all. She repeated that fact so many times that I wondered whether she was trying to remind me or herself.

I was fumbling to get my laptop bag into the passenger seat of my car one-handed when I snapped. 'You know, *I* also have a job that I value.'

She sighed. 'Prue, I'm sorry, babe. Tell me, what's the new job like?'

The problem was I couldn't tell her, mostly because I didn't yet know. 'It's a full manuscript query,' I said, because I knew that much at least. 'But I don't actually know much about the client. Her name is Ruby, she lives out in the sticks. Arthur said a lot of the information had come in from her legal person rather than the woman herself.'

'Legal person? Well, that sounds big?'

Arthur must have thought so, too, which would be why he'd offered me the work. He'd also told me not to fuck it up. The agency would clear a good commission from this project, providing I could win over the client on this first meeting.

'When's the first meeting?' Rita asked, sealing my suspicion that she hadn't listened to a word I'd said in the earlier part of this conversation. When I took a beat too long to answer, though, something must have clicked. 'You're currently rushing to get to your first meeting.'

'Ten points for Hufflepuff.'

'Fuck you, I'm absolutely not a–'

'You're that or you're a Slytherin. There's no way a friend from another house would make me late for a meeting.'

'Go. Be brilliant. Call me later and tell me everything?'

I'd signed a non-disclosure agreement already. Still, I said, 'Of course. You go and be brilliant, too, okay? Show 'em who's the lady boss.' Then I hung up before she could start again. The postcode for the property was already keyed into my navigation system so I geared up and pulled out, and hoped for a good bite.

The cottage looked like something from a fairy tale. There was a thatched roof, climbing vines, and the silhouette of a wicked witch watching me as I unloaded my car. I pretended not to see her. She was sizing me up, I guessed. She'd need a good measure of me before she put me in a pot to roast. Although in her position I would have probably done the same. Clients were also a little cagey with me to begin with, until they softened into whatever the work was. So while she looked over me, I looked over the property some more. The nearest neighbour wasn't within eyesight; I couldn't remember the last house I'd seen since driving through the village. Ruby mustn't be one for company, I decided. I pulled my phone out to check my signal bars – a precautionary measure – then padded toward the front door. There was a porchway packed with flowers and I wondered how much maintenance something like this must take. *Do you work, Ruby?* There were full-bloom roses forming a crown around the space and I was midway through studying their folds when the front door was snatched open. My hand flew to my chest on instinct, and from the fright. Still, I had to laugh.

'Ruby?' I held out a hand.

Her face softened as she reciprocated. 'Prudence?'

*Jesus. Only my mother.* 'Please, call me Prue.'

Ruby was an intimidatingly attractive woman; a reality that dawned on me when she gave me a full smile and welcomed me into her home. She had the kind of curls that *must* be natural because no hairdresser in the land could possibly replicate the wildness of them so fully. Her hair was dark brown and streaked with grey but in a way that suited her. She was in jeans that were worn through in places – another part of her that looked more authentic than it did designer – and a woollen jumper that covered her shape. Still, when she ran a hand through her hair I could see from slender fingers that Ruby must be a lean woman under her clothing. When I scooted past her and into the hallway, I caught a faint smell of smoke, too. Somewhat ironically, if I'd met Ruby under other circumstances then I would have guessed she was a writer – or at the very least an artist – from appearance alone.

She shut the door then, and walked past me down her hallway. 'I'll make us tea.'

'That would be great, thank you.' I lingered behind her a little. I wanted to look the place over for signs of artistry; clues about who Ruby was. I couldn't chase away the thought that there was something familiar about her and I wanted to hunt the walls down for clues. But after a slow meander along the first stretch of corridor I realised that I was going to be hard pushed to find anything. The photographs hung on the walls were all generic: prints that I recognised as part-famous, but they didn't say much about Ruby other than she liked portraits of beautiful women. *Are you hiding from me, Ruby?* I wondered whether the walls were always this discreet or whether she'd packed things away before I arrived. *Who are you?* 'Could I have a glass of water, too, please? That journey was a stuffy one.'

'You're welcome to take a walk outside if you want the air?'

I looked past her teatime preparations and out along the stretch of green. I caught sight of the cigarettes on the window then – *Ah, definitely a smoker* – but I let it go uncommented on.

'Maybe we can work out there?'

'Please. That's a lovely idea.'

I left Ruby to make drinks and wandered out into the garden. By the time she joined me, I already had parts of my portfolio spread out on the table, leaving just enough room for the cups and saucers she'd brought.

'I didn't know whether you had a preference on biscuits?' She was angled to head back inside.

'Oh, really, I'm okay. Why don't we just make a start? I'm really interested to know a little more about the project, if you're okay to jump in?' She flashed me a thin smile and sat. 'Counter to that, though, while we're talking through the project you're welcome to throw questions at me, too. I know this is a personal thing and I want you to feel you're in safe hands, if you decide to press forward with me as the writer.' I tried to flash the sweetest smile I could muster: candy canes on Valentine's Day sweet. I needed this win. 'You're welcome to take a browse and I can grab my laptop,' I was already reaching for it, 'to show you more.'

'Are you married?'

I was looking away, thank God, so she mustn't have caught my confused flicker. *Why are you asking that, Ruby?* 'No, I'm not married.' I clicked and scrolled through my laptop files to busy myself while I blitzed my history. 'No spouse, no children, although I do have a cat which is pretty close to the latter. No family to speak of. I've been working with the same agency for a long time now, though, so that's family to me in a lot of ways. I studied English and writing at university, and side-eye flirted with writing for a career. Not ghost-writing, admittedly, but I do love the work and the variety of projects I get is really good for me. I might write a real-life crime thriller one day, though, if I try hard enough.' It was littered with lies but it was the closest I was getting to the truth with a woman I didn't know.

I noticed Ruby's jaw clench. 'You want to write crime?'

'Something psychological.' I shrugged. 'One day.' I realised, then, that the drinks Ruby went to the effort of making had gone untouched, so I took a deliberate sip of my lukewarm tea and then leaned back into my patch of shade. 'But enough about me. What do I need to know about you?'

In the minutes that followed we established Ruby wasn't retired; she was just rich. She sold off land to buy the cottage and hide away from the world – *Why?* I wondered but didn't ask. – and she'd been living there for the last fifteen years or so, alone. When I asked her whether she was married, her right hand started to fiddle with her left in a way that answered the question for me. She wasn't divorced, though, but widowed. I listened attentively to it all and made the right noises, but there was still something about the woman I couldn't place. She reminded me of Mum, ever so slightly, in her appearance alone. But the way Ruby talked – deliberately, as though she was thumbing a thesaurus before she settled on a word – was different to the free-and-easy way Mum would have spoken. It's when she answered my question about her husband – 'He was murdered.' – that I finally realised what I was there for.

'That's what the book is about.'

She nodded slowly. 'Loosely, it's what I'd like the book to be about.'

I felt a real swell of sadness for Ruby then. *What a horrible topic for a memoir.* Although I couldn't help thinking, too, what a bloody brilliant project it would be to work on.

'I hope you don't mind me asking...'

'You want to know what happened,' she filled in the blank. 'If you're going to write about it then I suppose it's only fair. He went missing one evening. I thought he was out, that he'd be coming home, but he didn't. Instead, there was a search. It lasted days, I forget how many but,' she waved toward the house, 'I've got all the specifics. His body was discovered and there was eventually a trial. The suspect on trial was found not guilty and now, well, we're here.'

I skimmed back through what she'd given me. 'There are some blanks there.'

'I suppose the project is to fill those blanks in.'

'You mentioned a trial, a suspect?'

'A lengthy trial, actually.' She explained how the newspapers snatched up the story – *Is that why I recognise you, Ruby?* – and how every now and then some documentary-maker would announce an anniversary production to probe at her husband's death in more detail. *Christ,* I thought as she pressed on, *I hope I don't know any of those film-makers.* My circle of friends was limited to tortured artist types and an unsolved murder was everyone's favourite flavour of work now, wasn't it? 'Everyone loves the unsolved mystery of a middle-class man who was murdered in rural England. It gives the bloodhounds something to report on, and re-report on.' I nodded along. *Yep, I definitely know some of those bloodhounds.* 'But there are a lot of truths about the story that never saw the light of day, which I'm led to believe happens with cases like mine.'

'I think it's about time I started to take notes.' I tried to sound loose, easy, as I reached for my notebook. There was too much happening already and I needed to keep track. 'What was your husband's name, sorry, Ruby? I don't think you mentioned.'

She hesitated for so long that I looked up and caught her staring off into the garden.

'Ruby?'

Her head snapped round. 'Sorry. Ah, Roger Miller. His name was Roger.'

'Roger Miller,' I repeated and rolled the name around to get a flavour for it. But part of the surname got stuck in a tooth and while I was feeling around to loosen it, it suddenly struck me like a pulled wisdom. 'Which must mean the suspect on trial for his murder was... you?'

# CHAPTER SEVENTEEN

What's the word for when a murderer tells you they didn't do it?

She said the tea was cold and she needed something to warm her, then she left for the kitchen. I only murmured in agreement. When she'd gone, I checked my phone again and ignored the four WhatsApp messages that were waiting; I was only interested in the signal. If I needed to make an emergency call, to anyone, I needed to know my phone wouldn't crap out on me. Although she'd booked me through an agency, so she knew that people knew that I was–

'Fucking hell, Prue,' I whispered. 'Get yourself together.'

Sometimes it helped to hear things aloud.

I counted taps – one, two, three – of my index finger against my thigh and I took deep breaths – four, five, six – while I looked around the garden – seven, eight, nine. It really was beautiful. Not-Ruby must have put a lot of work into pruning and nurturing and other kind things you wouldn't necessarily expect a murderer to do. *Not that she is a murderer*, I reminded myself as I started the tapping cycle again and inhaled greedily. I thought I could smell smoke and I wondered whether she was using the tea break for a cigarette, too. Under normal circumstances I was only a social smoker but – I let out a sharp huff – I was sitting in the back garden of a woman tried for murdering her husband...

'An average day at the office,' I whispered again.

There were two rabbits hopping around each other at the bottom of the lawn and I wondered whether they knew whose garden they'd wandered into. Or whether they'd done it unknowingly as well.

'Biscuit?'

She pulled my attention around. 'Please,' I answered quickly, grateful at the prospect of having something easier to chew over. On the tea tray there was a plate of biscuits already: chocolate digestive; custard cream; bourbon; shortbread... But there was only one of each. My logic-brain told me she was being considerate, because she didn't know my preference still. Meanwhile, my crazy-brain: *What if you pick the biscuit she wants?*

'I must have given you quite a shock,' she said, as she poured my tea then her own. 'You'll have questions, I suspect, and I'm happy to answer them in some detail. Of course, more detail will come if you choose to accept the project.'

I liked that the onus was on me. Or maybe I liked that there was still a way out.

'To start with,' she carried on, 'I may as well re-introduce myself. You can call me Erica.'

I forced a laugh. 'Well, it's nice to re-meet you.' I knew I sounded nervous but fucking hell, who wouldn't be? 'Do you have a preference on biscuit?'

Erica seemed genuinely amused. 'I'm sorry. You've just found out that I was found not guilty for murdering my husband and you're asking about biscuits.' She nudged the plate towards me. 'There are full packets in the kitchen. Please, take whichever. Sugar is good for a shock.'

I took the bourbon, dunked it in my tea and caught it just in time before it collapsed. 'Thank you,' I said, with half the biscuit still to go. 'I feel a little...' I couldn't find the right word.

'Thrown?'

*That'll do.* 'I suppose.'

'Have another biscuit.' She sipped her tea and looked down the stretch of lawn. 'Roger was found washed up on the coast. He wasn't worlds away from where we lived at the time, but it certainly wasn't home, either. They asked me to explain how he got there.' She huffed out a half-arsed laugh. 'That was before they'd arrested me, or suspected me, even. They just seemed to think I should know. The time he'd spent in the water had ruined a lot of the evidence, I think.' She swallowed hard and I heard the glug from across the table, but I pretended not to notice. Instead, I reached for the chocolate digestive; dipped and ate and stared at her, like I was a hungry kid at an adult story-time. 'That actually helped their case against me in the end; the fact that the only evidence they could find on him was evidence that somehow linked him to me. My lawyer argued that of course it tied him to me; we lived together. But,' she waved away that part of the story, too, 'we can talk that through in more detail.

'During the autopsy they found substantial damage to his head. They went back and forth on whether it could have happened in the water. In the end, though, they decided that someone must have...' Erica paused and pulled in a deep inhale; I thought I heard her wheeze. Whether or not she'd killed him, this mustn't be an easy story to tell. *Christ, did you kill him though?* I couldn't switch off from the thought so I did the only sensible thing I could and stuffed another biscuit in my mouth instead: custard cream. 'They decided on blunt force trauma.'

She reached to tap the back of her head. 'Somewhere around here.'

I froze mid-chew as the absurdity of the situation hit me with a – well, a blunt force.

'When they eventually decided I must have done it, after a hundred interviews or more, I was remanded in custody. I'm told there's no way around that for suspected murderers which I suppose is fair.' She made the same huffing noise again. 'Or rather, it's fair when they've got the right person in custody. Less so, otherwise. After that period, though, there was a decision made that I didn't pose a flight risk or a risk to society at large.'

'That's how it works with murder?' I asked, sans tact of any kind.

'If you plan to kill a spouse, what risk are you once that spouse is dead?' She sipped her tea but held eye contact with me over the rim of the porcelain. I didn't like that. 'Meanwhile, if you're a drug lord or a – Christ, I don't know. If you're something *worse* than someone who might have murdered their husband in a blind rage one night, then you're more likely to hurt more people, commit more crime, and so on. I had a very good lawyer who explained things in much better terms. He was a lot more eloquent.'

'It's okay, I get the gist.' I reached forward to take another biscuit, but my fingers crushed up against the empty plate. 'Oh.'

Erica looked around and smiled. 'Do you have a preference now?'

'Oh, really, you don't need to...' I started to protest but she was already standing up, plate in hand. 'Whatever you come to first is fine, thank you. God, I'm so sorry, you must think I'm a total animal.' I laughed and I was pleased to see her match the amusement.

'Not at all. You need the sugar.'

She said it with such certainty that I wondered how many more shocks were coming.

When Erica had topped up tea – and my blood sugar – she skipped ahead to the real meat of the case. 'The fucking bloodhounds,' she said, with so much venom in her that I had to make a real effort not to recoil. After all, I'd been one such bloodhound in my time. Instead, I shoved a shortbread triangle into my mouth and chewed through her explanation of how Roger was painted as a saint in the media, while she was painted as the whore. One newspaper after another talked through Roger's money, his business endeavours, his loyalty to Erica; while others talked through Erica's misdemeanours, mistakes she'd made when she was younger.

'Among many other things that never bloody happened.' She kneaded at her chest as she spoke, and I wondered how anxious all this old ground must have made her. 'I don't want to trash-talk the British press in the book, incidentally. I only want to correct things that should have been researched better the first time around. There's a lot of information the press might have got right if they'd thought only to ask the right people. Besides, do you know how difficult it is to keep telling the same story when everyone around you is changing theirs the whole while?'

I sensed the question was rhetorical but, still. 'What do you mean?'

'The police, how often the police were asking the same things. How often I was having to remember what I'd said,' she explained. But it seemed a strange way of phrasing it... 'I only mean to say the press were intervening, and complicating. There were a lot of contrary stories that ran hard against my own and it made it all the more challenging to find people who would believe what I was saying.' She sighed, wheezed. 'Many people now still don't.'

'Do you mind if I ask about your choice to leave the city?' I wasn't taking notes anymore; I was only curious. Erica was looking down the length of the garden when she nodded. 'It sounds as though it's been a while since you had contact with anything to do with the case. In terms of press coverage, media, that sort of thing. Was that your plan, when you came here, to isolate yourself like that?'

She turned to collect her tea. Then she did that same thing again, where she watched me from over its rim as she drank. 'Isolation is a funny word to use for all this.'

'What word would you use?'

She thought for a second. 'Peace.'

We swapped a smile, then, and it occurred to me how dreadfully lonely Erica must have been after everything, to opt for this as a happy alternative. 'I think that kind of answers my question.'

The light in the garden changed. I didn't look up, but it was the grey-sudden-chill that comes with cloud coverage. I noticed Erica shudder at the temperature drop. It was the first time in a while that I'd thought to check my watch. When I did, though, I realised another ninety minutes had passed and there was a staff meeting back in the city that I was dangerously close to missing. Although talking to an accused murderess was certainly more interesting than anything waiting at the office.

'We should move inside,' Erica said, pulling closed her cardigan.

'I should actually be making a move. I've taken up so much of your time already.'

'Nonsense. It's my time to spend, Prue. If you need to go, though, then please don't feel the need to make an excuse.' I looked up from packing my notebook away. 'I'll walk to your car?'

'Thank you, Erica. This has been...' I felt around blindly for an adjective.

She laughed. 'Interesting, I suspect.'

'Yes, interesting is exactly what it's been.'

*So interesting that I'm dying inside over not being able to tell my friends...*

Erica walked me back through the cottage with a long and winding explanation about how old the building was. She said there had been workmen in and out over the years, bringing the place up to standard. 'It's something I hope the next owners will appreciate anyway.' She opened the front door then. 'Prue, it's been a pleasure.'

She offered her hand, and I accepted, but I wasn't quite over what she'd said. 'Are you leaving?' Erica threw me a puzzled look. 'The next owners, you said. I didn't see a For Sale sign on the drive up here.'

'Oh,' she waved the comment away, 'I only meant hypothetically, one day.'

'Ah, I see. Well, I'm sure when you sell up for pastures new, someone will love it as much as you have. But listen, all of this has been so interesting, so thank you for meeting with me. I have a few things to talk through with my manager at the agency and–'

'Not too many things though.' She cut across me and I loitered on whether it was a comment or a question. 'The paperwork.'

I caught her meaning then. 'Of course, not too many things.'

'Remember this is entirely your decision as well, won't you?'

'Whether I take the job, do you mean?'

'Of course. I realise it's a specialist area. Lots of cloak and dagger work, potentially.' She laughed again. 'There might be a better phrase than that, given the circumstances, but you catch my meaning, I should think. I only suspect working on a book is one thing, never mind a book wrapped up in so many complexities as this one.'

I thanked her for the kind warning about the hard work ahead; not that it made a bit of difference. Then I promptly turned and headed for the car. She waved me off from the front porch, where she was leaning against the open doorway. There was a cool breeze building that took tendrils of her hair away with it, and I saw a flash of Medusa about her when I glanced back. I didn't look for long in case she managed to turn me to stone and fix me to the spot. But I waved to her reflection in my rear-view mirror after I'd manoeuvred down her driveway. In my head I counted out an appropriate number of days to call her and accept the job. I didn't want to seem too eager. But I wasn't prepared to lose out on her courtship either.

# CHAPTER EIGHTEEN

What's a better word for fame-hungry?

I didn't have the chance to talk to Arthur in private, not around the staff meeting that I'd rushed back to the city for. Still, the day after I met Erica I had to go into the office to drop off the final stretches of paperwork for another job I'd taken. That's when Arthur cornered me at the photocopier when I'd hardly been in the building for five minutes. I heard the slurp of his coffee before I saw him; the noise was unmistakable.

'We talked about the slurping.' I lifted out one sheet, replaced it with another.

'Hey, I'm the boss.' He took another sip and, I thought, made a point of slurping even louder. 'I'll slurp if I want to.'

'Ah, the lesser-known Lesley Gore number.'

He snorted. 'You're not old enough to know who Lesley Gore is.'

I hummed the opening bars to 'It's My Party'. 'What's up, Arthur? What's the news?'

'I was hoping you could tell me. Got a second?' He nodded in the general direction of his office. 'It would be good to hear about your meeting yesterday, if there's anything you can share slash anything I need to know.' Arthur was the only person I knew who input slashes into his dialogue. He didn't wait for a reply, only turned and trod the way. I hurriedly collected my sheets of paper and followed dotingly, like all his writers were expected to. 'Close the door?' he said when we were inside the space. 'Pull up a pew, kid. What do *you* know?'

'I know there's an NDA in place that means I can't tell you about the client.'

'No, but you can tell me about the meeting.'

I rolled the options around in my head. *How much was too much?* 'Look, I'm going to ask you something but before I ask, I want you to know that I've already decided I'm taking the job.'

'Oh-kaaaay.'

'Would you ever work with a criminal?'

His eyes widened. 'My, you did get a juicy one. Well, in truth, I have worked with criminals. Not in ghost-writing or editing. But in my journo days I spent a fair bit of time with some hard-edged individuals, yes. Did it bother me? Absolutely not. There's a story to tell and it was literally my job to tell it, so I cracked on.'

'What kind of criminals?'

'Drugs, mostly, the occasional bit of gang work. What kind of criminal?'

'I can't answer that without breaking the–'

'Yeah, yeah.' He waved my professionalism away. 'Look, Prue, all I'll say is that you need to, first and foremost, make sure you're being safe. Secondly, make sure you're making a wise move for your career. No one will know you've written this book, necessarily, but you need to ask yourself whether, let's say, someone *did* know you'd written the book. How would you feel? Ashamed, or proud?'

*I'd feel like I could cash in.* But I didn't admit that thought aloud. 'Okay, that actually helps.'

'Do you already know the answer then?'

I smirked. 'The same answer it's been all along.'

That afternoon I bulk-ordered Erica Miller biographies for next-day delivery. Two days on from the meeting and Amazon was exclusively suggesting true-crime publications in their advertisement emails to me. I still hadn't called her. The phone call was on a future to-do list because even though I knew I wouldn't change my mind, I wasn't prepared to go into a gunfight without ammunition either. I turned my phone off for a full day and made it my mission to learn everything I could about the woman. In each book she was described as a villain, a caricature of the Wicked Witch we'd all been warned about so many times. But there was nothing I could find that married well with the woman I'd met days before.

Her marriage to Roger had been blissful/rocky/hard to find out much about; they'd met at university/in a pub/through friends; they hadn't had children because Erica couldn't get pregnant/Erica didn't want them/Erica couldn't carry to term. I snorted at the mis-details around their child status.

'Of course it would be the woman's fault.'

By the time I'd cross-referenced where they met and how long they'd been married, I was already starting to question the quality of the books I'd bought. There was so much information that mismatched and I couldn't reason with how few truths were avail–

My front doorbell buzzed an interruption.

'Shit.' I checked my watch. *Rita.*

I hurried to pack away the books that were splayed around the living room. The space was a mess of broken spines and dog-eared pages; post-its and scribbled discrepancies to be fact-checked. I was going to need a better filing system. Rita waits for no woman, though, and I'd just about managed to rush everything into a nearby drawer when she hit the buzzer outside again.

'Jesus, give a woman a chance to get decent,' I said as I opened the door.

'Well, that explains the wait.' She leaned forward, kissed my cheek and pushed past into my living room. 'Max is sad so I brought him.'

He trailed in behind her and kissed my cheek, too. That was the kind of cliché we were.

'I'm not sad.'

'Babe, there's no shame in being sad.'

I shut the door and followed them in. 'Why are you sad, Max?'

'Fuck sake, I'm not–'

'He's sad because he lost a job, because he bid too high, because he's *greedy*.' Rita was her usual sympathetic self. She didn't have much time for compassion; unless she was trying to elicit it from others. 'How did your meeting go?'

Max and I swapped a look. 'I'm sorry, is that it? Have we finished talking about him?'

'Apparently.' Max laughed, but there was hurt on his face. It was hard, working in our industries, especially in this day and age. Max was a photographer, too, although he specialised in commissioned works, which essentially meant it was even harder for him to come by work. 'I lost a job, that really is it, and I'm not sad; I'm just disappointed.'

Rita held her palm up to him, closed her eyes and set her free hand on her forehead. She moved her open hand around, as though sensing something in the space. 'Mother, is that you?'

I slapped her arm. 'Don't be a cow.'

'She can't help it.' Max raised an eyebrow at Rita who

bobbed her tongue out in response. 'Tell us about your meeting?' he asked.

'I actually can't.' I dropped onto the beanbag opposite them both. 'NDA.'

'For a meeting?' Rita was hooked. 'Isn't that usually something that happens *after*?'

'It depends on the client.'

'And you've got one that's *really* ghostly?' Max chimed in. I noticed him inch forward.

I couldn't help but glance toward the drawer where Erica was stashed. 'Yes.'

They whooped and whistled. 'How juicy are we talking? Career-defining?' Rita asked.

'Rita, shut up. I'm a ghost-writer. What about this could be career-defining?'

'It could be leaked.' She raised an eyebrow. 'Someone could out you as the writer behind...' She waited for me to fill in the blank but I only shook my head.

'Nice try.'

'Seriously,' Max tried a softer tone with me, 'a secret client must mean big money?'

It was big money – with the potential to be bigger. Erica had put a rough draft figure at the bottom of the non-disclosure for our meeting and it was more than I'd been paid for a job in... ever. It was enough to clear a chunk of debt and keep a roof over my head, and maybe clear a little more debt besides. *God knows there's enough to be cleared.* In fact, the money was such a swing vote that I'd opted against even telling Connie, my sister that is, about the job offer. Granted, I couldn't tell her much. But I knew that if she got a whiff of the sum she would have sniffed me down and pinned me with a loaded barrel until the book was written. *She has her own reasons though...*

Max leaned further forward to set a hand on my shoulder. 'Are you with us?'

I laughed. 'Christ, sorry. It's been a heavy research day.' I struggled to get up from the small beads shifting about beneath my weight with every move. Once I was upright, though, I straightened my T-shirt out and slapped on a smile. 'It's a big sum and a big job and I'm going to take it, and that's as much as I'm going to say. Now, are we on wine or coffee?'

'Wine,' they said in synchronicity, so I left to uncork a bottle of red.

I made a show of banging cupboards and clinking glasses, a mirage of being busy, while I waited for my phone to turn on. I slammed the fridge door closed, rustled packets of snacks and shouted, 'Just letting it breathe!' Then I held on for Erica's voicemail service to take over from the ringing. At the beep I recorded, 'Miss Miller, it's Prue Carr from the agency. I've given the job some real thought over the last few days and long story short, if you'll have me then I'm on board.'

## CHAPTER NINETEEN

What's another word for suspicious?

I was already chewing my way through my second bourbon biscuit when Erica mentioned 'ground rules'. The term made me feel like a teenager staying with a stern family friend. But I nodded my understanding all the same and concentrated on not getting biscuit crumbs on the sofa while she listed them off. I reached into my bag without even looking and felt around for my recorder. It was normally the sort of thing I'd do on my mobile, tablet, laptop, or another newfangled device. But all of that was hooked up to the cloud and I thought Erica would need more security than that. She struck me as sheepish that first day and I wondered whether it was because we were getting down to the grit of the deal.

'I don't want anything recorded,' she snapped.

'I'm sorry?' There was still biscuit in my mouth and I was conscious of sprayed flecks, but I couldn't hold back. '*Nothing*, like, at all?'

She shook her head. 'You're comfortable making notes? Or you looked it the other day.'

'This is a long project to get through on notes alone.'

'I'll give you time to catch up. In fact, that's one of the other rules. We'll never do two days in a row of talking. It will be too much for us both, I think. Do you have any other work commitments at the moment or will you be focused singly on this one?'

I knew the right answer. 'Only this.' A flicker of a smile danced over Erica's face and she nodded. 'I actually only do one long-form project at a time. But if you need for me to write everything in notes, or handwritten accounts, long-form, then having a day between things will be helpful for getting information typed up.'

'You'll type everything?'

'It helps to have a digital record.' No sooner was the explanation out and it occurred to me: *That's why she doesn't want anything recorded.* I tried to keep my face neutral but the only way I could manage it was to fill it with something. 'May I?' I pointed to the biscuit plate again and it hit me that I hadn't asked permission before taking the first two. *Will she see that as suspicious?*

She laughed. 'Please. I'm not much of a biscuit fan.'

'Well,' I spoke around the first bite of a chocolate digestive, 'I clearly am.'

If I were going to be working with Erica for months on end, I was going to need a better coping mechanism than shoving a biscuit in my face every time something surprised me – lest I leave the project with diabetes. It seemed likely, too, that there were more shocks coming. *So if you think it's bad now,* I told myself as I chewed and waited for her to add something more, but she didn't.

'Next?' I prompted her.

'I don't want you to do any research.'

*Thank God for this biscuit…*

'Not any?'

'Nothing beyond the information that I'll give you.' She sipped her tea with deliberate slowness as though giving me an opening, but I didn't take it. 'The book isn't about the information that's already out there, Prue. If I wanted a book about the information that's available then I'd dip into the biographies and transcripts and podcasts and – God, however many other productions there are about me, or Roger, or the pair of us. There's a wealth of utter crap available about what happened. Pardon my language, will you? The book isn't about what I did, or what people *say* that I did. The book should be about the things I didn't do; the things they've told everyone that I did, but I didn't.'

I had to give it to her; it made sense. While I finished chewing, I quickly reasoned that the biographies that were already stashed away in my living room like contraband goods – which of course, they now were – didn't have anything to do with this rule though. I'd bought them *before* the research ban was imposed so I'd keep them and read them and…

'Okay, that all sounds reasonable.' I'd agree with anything Erica said. She was a hard-faced woman to risk a disagreement with. 'Well,' I rooted around for my notebook and stashed the digital recorder away, 'let's get started?'

Erica struggled to unfold herself from the sofa. She was wearing leggings that showed the shape of her legs and I was struck by how slim they were; it was no wonder that she wobbled slightly when she stood. 'Cramp,' she said and laughed the struggle away. But I'd noticed more than once already how her body looked to pain her in a way that didn't seem quite right for her age. I hadn't done the maths exactly, but Erica couldn't be older than my own mother would have been. Her hair was fixed in a messy bun that day, low down the back of her head, but there were curls escaping. The way she moved with purpose reminded me of Mum a little, too, or at least what I remembered of her.

Erica tucked herself out of sight behind my sofa. 'There are a few things here that might be helpful.' When she came back into my line of sight, she was dragging a heavy chest; one designed to look like a stack of books. It was a novelty item and a detail that I couldn't quite marry with the class that Erica put across. 'Roger bought this,' she said as she tugged it further into the centre of the room. 'It's full of... I suppose you'd call it memorabilia.'

Suspicious; watchful; cautious. I counted through synonyms while I unbuckled the case. Sceptical; wary; careful. Then I peered under the lid like a wild creature might leap out. Apprehensive – I ran a finger along the spines of thick folders – quizzical – and parted them like lips opening to scream out secrets – suspecting – which was when I saw they were tabbed up, post-it notes displaying their titles. Mistrustful.

'Newspapers?' I looked up and caught a nod. But then I dove back in. I pulled out the first folder my fingers happened to land on, which had *The Sun and Star* written across the front. I licked a finger, then, to part the thick parchment of the pages inside and skimmed one after another, gently easing them apart where age had brought their adhesive together. The folder was made up of newspaper clippings, articles that had Erica's name in the headlines – or, I soon saw, Roger's. There were monikers, too, names that mightn't mean anything unless you knew who they were about; which of course I now did. Murderous Miller dominated headliners; Hungry for Husband's Inheritance; Hiding from Judgement?

'Are they scrapbooks?' I lifted the first folder out of my way and greedily reached for a second one. *Why does she have these?* I wondered as I repeated the process with a second set of articles, stripped from a second newspaper. In this one, the pages were yellowed and there was a faint smell of smoke lifting from the book, too. *When did she make them?* I was halfway through the second book when I realised she hadn't answered. When I looked up Erica was perched opposite me, balanced on the edge of her sofa rather than nestled into it as she had been earlier. 'These folders,' I pushed, 'they're everything they wrote about you?'

She reached over for the book I'd already set to one side and skimmed a page.

'This is everything.' There was a lot of dead air in the room while she skimmed and I skimmed, the only sound between us, then, was the synchronicity of our pages turning. I don't know what headline she read, but there was a snort from the across the room that caught my attention. 'Well, everything except the things I actually did.'

I tried to do a headcount of the folders. But by the time I'd got to ten, I thought to ask another question. 'Is this actually everything or is there more?'

She raised an eyebrow. 'Greedy?'

I tried to laugh. 'Curious.' *Suspicious,* I thought, and suddenly a little worried, too. It looked like hours of work had gone into documenting the memories Erica should have wanted to forget. *Why would someone hold onto these allegations?* I wondered. But, while the folders had sent me feeling nervous, it still didn't make a comment one way or another on her guilt. *Whether she killed her husband or not, though, this is still weird...* Not that I was/wasn't exactly convinced she *had* killed him, or I wouldn't be drinking her tea and eating her biscuits.

'There are more things we can use but I should think this will give us a good start.'

'I'll say.'

'Are you okay?' she asked, and I knew, then, that I needed to up my poker face.

'Stunned, but in a very good way. When you said I couldn't do research, well… it goes against the journalist in me.' I laughed and it at least raised a smile in her. 'But this is all going to be really helpful. You don't mind me rifling through?'

'Please.' She set her hands on her knees and lifted herself up easier than she had earlier. 'Help yourself. But I'm working on an empty stomach so I think I'll freshen up that biscuit plate, if you don't mind a break. Tea?'

'Could I have something colder?'

She smiled. 'Home-made lemonade?'

I would have preferred something from a bottle, but sure. What choice was there? 'Thank you.' She was halfway out the room already so I spoke to her back. 'Erica, the ledgers. Could I take them—'

'No.' She hovered for a moment, as though expecting a protest on my part.

Instead, I did my best to stifle a sigh and went back to *Your Local*'s exposé on Erica Miller. Like any disobedient child, I waited until I could hear the whistle of water and the clink of crockery before I made my move. In the dim light of the living room, I stood and took an aerial shot of the books splayed out, a close-up of them in their chest, and then a series of closer ones still, showing what they were archiving. I managed to photograph one or two individual articles, but I knew the names of the papers would give me my best starting point for – *what?* I reminded myself that I wasn't meant to be doing research beyond what Erica had given me. I took a few general shots of the room then, too, and with the nose of a journalist told myself, surely, she had given me all of this?

By the time she walked back in, carrying a tall glass of

lemonade complete with ice and a slim wedge of lime, my phone was stashed inside my bag. It sat alongside the digital recorder that, unfortunately, must have got switched on by mistake when I'd stashed it away...

# CHAPTER TWENTY

What's the word for a missing best friend?

After I'd asked Erica about her moniker for meeting with me, the name Ruby Brinkley came to hover over the rest of our time together like a disgruntled spectre. Erica told me not to look; promised that even if I did, I wouldn't find. But like a child who's been told not to think of a pink elephant, the image ballooned into something circus-like, and it occupied my mind like nothing else she and I had talked about. By the time we were wrapping up our Ruby session – as I noted it down – everything in me wanted out of the cottage. If Erica sensed that, then she at least had the decency not to comment on it. Given her track record, I wondered how often people had hurriedly packed their bags and fled her company. There was nearly a pang of guilt then, for how quick I was to think ill of her, like so many others had. But she didn't exactly make it easy to feel comfortable sometimes.

'Thanks for today,' I said, trying to hold the tremor in my voice. 'Really interesting stuff.'

She caught my arm as I stepped over the threshold. 'Ruby is fine.' There was an audible churn in my stomach. I wanted to pass it off as hunger but there were two emptied biscuit plates in the living room that would have made a liar of me. 'I meant what I said about people looking to make a monster of me, Prue. But did you mean what you said, about seeing nothing monstrous?'

I smiled. *Apparently I'm not the only who makes notes.* 'I haven't seen anything monstrous.' I chose my words carefully; this wasn't a lie. Erica had shown me *strange* and *suspicious* but making her into a monster from that would be a stretch. 'You're the client, though, and what you say has to go. So if you tell me not to research something, well...' I shrugged. I knew that if I finished the sentence I'd be lying.

Instead of typing up my notes from the previous day's interview, I waded through the remaining Erica biographies that were dotted around the apartment. There was no mention of Ruby in any of them. But I couldn't work out whether I'd expected there to be. Late that night, after a string of dead ends from my paperback research, I tapped out a text – "Dear Erica. Not feeling too well. Could we please postpone tomorrow? Best. P." – and quietly allotted myself a second day to research the missing friend. With enough time, I knew there must be something hidden in a corner of the world that would answer the question of Ruby. I'd start with the internet, the source of all knowledge, and work my way out from sources I found there. If I could just find a lead then–

The chirp of my phone cut through the plan: Erica.

'Hello.' I tried to sound croaky, although I hadn't decided what was wrong with me yet.

'Prue? It's Erica. You're sick?'

'Oh, I'm sure it's nothing, I–'

'Do you have someone there?' she interrupted me.

'I'm sorry?'

'To look after you. Do you have someone there?'

'Oh.' *Oh, the guilt.* There was an influx of bad feeling in my stomach. Here I was, lying to her so I could investigate her missing best friend. There she was, being all motherly. 'I'm on my own at the moment but I have a friend on the way over with supplies.' The lie came easily without me even thinking and I wondered whether it was some kind of self-defence mechanism; a survival instinct. 'But honestly, I think it's just a migraine brewing. I get them from time to time. It's nothing that a day in a darkened room won't set right.'

'Okay.' There was a long pause. 'Well, get some rest. Be mindful of screen time, won't you?' She ended the call while I was busy deciding whether it was a pointed comment or not. The next time I cancelled, I'd call.

That night I fell asleep, phone in hand, with a search engine open for "Ruby Brinkley Erica Miller". It was an uninspired starting point, so it wasn't altogether surprising – the morning after the night before – when I woke and scrolled and saw that the first three pages of results hadn't produced any offerings either. I dragged myself from bedroom to kitchen to beanbag; with coffee, laptop and mobile in tow, all the while wondering, *where to start...* While I waited for my laptop to warm up I checked my phone and skimmed the various group chats to make sure I hadn't missed anything there, then I knocked the handset into airplane mode.

There was a document saved to my desktop with all the basics of Erica. With a click and a scroll I decided on a starting point: Regent's Hall. From family to family there might be no trace, but I reasoned a school as well-respected as Regent's Hall had to have some archival materials in its back pocket. If I were lucky, I thought, with a fresh browser open, there'd be at the very least an alumni list.

'Bingo.'

Across the top of the homepage for the school's website

there were a number of headings, including: 'From Past to Present'. I clicked into the page and selected the first of Erica's school years from the drop-down menu. There wasn't a list of students, but there were images; one after the other in black and white to begin with but slowly growing colours as the images became more modern, and the equipment used to take them more advanced. The students were itemised across the bottom of each photograph, too: "Our girls, from left to right..." but I didn't spot Ruby on the first page, or the second. It took longer than expected, even, to find Erica. But I did eventually. She was the prettiest girl in each picture and I wondered how much her peers must have hated her for that. Her hair was fairer when she was younger, curled in more of a corkscrew way than how she wore it now. There was something in her expression, though, that looked exactly the same. Whether she was smiling or making a neutral face for a class portrait, there was something of Erica that I recognised from the past against the woman I'd been working with – and neither version looked monstrous.

'Oh, but the monsters never do,' I said with another scroll.

It wasn't until page seven that my search finally turned up something helpful.

'There you are...'

Up to that point, Erica's beauty had gone unrivalled. But there was something about Ruby. The pair were often photographed together, which made their prettiness even more apparent. Ruby's hair was a deep auburn, dead straight and trailing down to her stomach – or her back, in the action-shot photos of her on the sports field. While Erica was tall and slim, Ruby was a good three inches shorter with an hourglass silhouette that showed even through the sack of her school uniform. They were markedly different in so many ways. But whether it was their confidence, their charisma, or the fact that they both held direct eye contact with the camera – with *me*, the voyeur – there was certainly something about them. I could only imagine the trouble they would have either tumbled into or deliberately stirred up had they been unleashed on unsuspecting pupils from a rival boys school.

I saved the web addresses for a handful of images in the hope that they might prove useful further down the line, then I continued in my search. For months on end the two were inseparable at every school occasion until... No Ruby.

'Come on, come on. People don't just disappear.'

I looked deeper into the archive but there really was nothing. I scrolled for so long that eventually Erica disappeared, too, long past the point of having graduated from her school years. For a handful of terms that followed I dipped in and out, reasoning Ruby might have been held back a year; maybe she dropped out and rejoined a different class sometime later. But no, the couple were entirely wiped out of the photographed history for that particular haystack. Which left me with nothing more than a handful of images to start searching out from.

That, and Ruby's name. Her surname was one I hadn't come across before. But Erica hadn't told me anything about her friend's parents. Still, knowing that Ruby had gone to Regent's Hall was evidence enough to tell me her family came from money. So I restarted my search. There was a Brinkley accountancy company listed nearby to where Erica and Ruby both attended school, closely followed by a Brinkley solicitors' firm. Both were still up and running, too, with positive reviews showing from previous clients. There were newspaper articles attached to them, high-profile cases, an admirable track record apiece. So I worked out, starting with William – the man listed as owner and founder of the accountancy firm – followed by Elsa – the other founder of the solicitors, although one of my first searches showed me that she was no longer practising at the firm.

'But I suppose you wouldn't be,' I realised, remembering the maths of their ages.

William looked to have taken a step back as well, although he was marketed as the face of the 'family company'. For a family firm, though, there was little about William's actual family listed on the site. Apparently he inherited the maths-and-numbers gene from his own father and he went on to train a man described as being like a son to him. Although, no mention of a daughter. Whoever the like-a-son was, though, he looked to be the head of the company for now, aside from the photo ops that William was brought in for. When I reached the bottom of their About Us page I spotted a landline number. *What can it hurt?* I thought then, after my strong sequence of dead ends and non-leads. *Another false start won't matter much.*

My phone buzzed alive with messages I'd missed over the morning when I turned it back on but I ignored them, and thumbed in the phone number instead. There were three low rings before...

'Good morning, Brinkley Accountancy. How may I help you?'

'Hi there,' I started, a hand to my forehead as I realised I didn't have a clue where to go next. 'I'm trying to get in touch with a Mr William Brinkley, I understand he's the CEO and founder of your firm.'

'Oh, he is, but I'm afraid Mr Brinkley isn't actually available at the moment. I can put you on hold for Mr McCroy, if it's anything he might be able to assist with?'

Mr McCroy, aka Like-A-Son. 'If you could, that would be great.'

I'd been on hold for nearly a minute when a man with a husky sound answered. 'Mr McCroy speaking, how may I help you?'

'Hi there, Mr McCroy, thanks so much for your time. I was

hoping to get in touch with Mr Brinkley regarding a woman who I think is his daughter.' It was a bold move but what was there to lose? 'I've been able to track her down through school records but I'm afraid I'm turning up a lot of loose ends. One or two searches have led me back to the Brinkleys' firm but it doesn't look as though there's a Ruby listed as being involved–'

'You're looking for a Ruby Brinkley?'

He used such a tone that I felt guilty for even admitting it. 'Yes.'

'Mr Brinkley won't be able to help you with that.'

There was something particular about the way he'd chosen his words. 'Okay, is it something you might be able to help me with then?' I tried instead.

He sighed. 'No one at this firm will be able to help you, I'm afraid.' There was long pause after he spoke, although it didn't sound like he'd quite finished. I heard someone talk in the background; an unrelated summons to a meeting more important than my mere mortal phone call could claim to be. 'I'm sorry, I didn't quite get your name there, but friend to friend, I can tell you not to bother trying Mrs Brinkley with this either. Neither of them will be able to help. You take care now.'

I'd hardly managed for a puff of air to escape my gaping mouth, never mind a follow-up question. The line went dead so fast that it took me a second to register what had happened. But I was pretty sure that, friend to friend, I hadn't found a pal who would help me.

# CHAPTER TWENTY-ONE

What's the word for staying on someone's good side; to stay safe?

Erica struck me as the kind of person worth keeping on the better side of. Whether or not she'd killed her husband – a claim I went back and forth on believing – I knew for certain she could make a woman disappear if she wanted to. Ruby couldn't be found, no matter the stone I checked under, which also meant that Erica's story about Ruby couldn't be shaken loose. I didn't have another option but to believe her. But of course, it made me all the more wary. I decided, then, it was worth playing nice as best as I could and playing suspicious in my own time.

In my visits after, we started by bonding over a Mothering Sunday meal; although Connie hadn't been impressed when I'd called to cancel my part in the visit to Mum's grave. 'She's a client, why is she even calling you on a Sunday?' she'd asked, her tone spiteful. In truth, I didn't know why Erica had called, or why she'd offered to buy me lunch. But there'd been something in her voice – 'I'm sorry if I've disturbed...' – that had made me wonder whether she needed me for something. Companionship, it turned out. She needed me for a walk into the village, to share a laugh with, to introduce me to a handful of local busybodies. If Erica had been a man, I would have felt like a trophy-piece.

Since, we'd shared the intimacy of a long day at work in front of a burning fire. But Erica was tired that day, and when she got tired I noticed she often lost things.

'It might have been January, when I had the procedure.' She pressed her fingers hard into her forehead as though she could knead the information loose. 'Or was it January when I met...'

'Are you okay, Erica?'

Her head snapped up. 'Of course.'

'You look a little... tired.'

I had learnt, too, that when Erica needed a rest, one had to be taken. It didn't matter how well she thought she'd hidden the illness. There was something rattling at the bars of her ribcage whenever she coughed; a sickness that unfolded from the sofa with her, set its hand on her hunched shoulders as she moved. Though, even in these moments, she was beautiful still. She tapped a beat against her chest and I wondered whether she were keeping time with her heart. Her other hand reached for her hair to push curls away from her face; they'd crept loose over the afternoon and there was something of the artist about her. *What would you have done with your classics education?* Not for the first time, I wondered what Erica's life might have been had she been surrounded by different men. But the sentimentality of that was something I was mindful of; could-have-beens wasn't what I was being paid for.

'Do you think we should take a break?' I asked.

'But I like us talking.'

'Well, I can stay.' I pushed my notebook to one side. I hadn't brought my laptop with me; I hardly ever did. Erica preferred everything to be handwritten. I think she liked the struggle of someone trying to keep up with her. Still, there were notes I could carry on making; chapter headings I could decide on. *Rooms I could look in.* 'If you rest now, you'll be awake for dinner. We don't have to talk about the book at all.'

'You'll stay just to talk?'

'And eat.' I laughed and she forced a smile, but that made the tiredness crack through more. 'I'll see what deliveries we can get in the countryside. You just rest. I'll be down here.'

Erica followed instructions like I'd never seen her do before. I wondered when someone had last cared for her. *Had Roger?* But it was another sentimental aside that I'd have to save for a different time. I didn't know how long her rest might last but there would only be so much open access granted by her sleeping, only a flight of stairs away. I waited until I heard the creak of a door opening and the click of it being closed before I crept from the living room. Downstairs, I only knew where the kitchen was, the dining room; she'd shown me the unused study, too, but she'd steadfastly ignored giving me details of "the box room".

'Junk, is it?' I'd asked.

She'd lingered. 'Something like that.'

The door opened without a rasp. I wondered how often the hinges were used. I lit the space using the torch on my iPhone and hurried inside as best as I could, squeezing myself between stacked boxes. *So it really is junk,* I thought as I scanned the miscellaneous terms that had been scribbled on the sides of each container. The hope and promise I'd felt for the room had dipped to a lukewarm disappointment until: WEDDING. The box was wedged up a far corner. If anyone had taken a quick scan of the space, they would have missed it. *Fortunate that I'm so thorough.* I teased at the corners of tape, but the seal came away easily; the adhesive loosened from years and dust. At a glance it only was a box of memories. I pulled out a small bag of party favours; scentless, but it crackled still at a touch. There were place settings marked 'bride' and 'groom', their cardboard yellowed and stained. Then, the garter; I thumbed the lace that had once been wrapped around young Erica's thigh and I tried not to get weighed down by the image. Further down, still, there were fabric samples: one white and crisp, *for a wedding dress?* The other looked like a rough cut taken from a suit. My fingers knocked against the plastic of a Tupperware box that housed a small bride and groom set, and a slab of icing skinned from a cake. I was partway through studying the wife for a likeness to Erica when there was a shift in the building; a noise from somewhere upstairs. I froze, spotlight still shining on the evidence. But there wasn't a follow-up sound.

I forced my mouth into an O and exhaled a nervous breath. *Move quicker, Carr, move...*

At the bottom of the box, I found the least surprising but most valuable item of the lot: a scrapbook. It was a different front cover to the ones in Erica's storage box. Those, plain black and distinguishable only from their post-it labels. This, white and cream and lace, earmarked as a wedding memento from the italicised writing on the front that shouted the occasion. It was thick and well-weighted with slips of paper bursting from the pages, so I took great care in opening the thing. Erica hadn't spoken, yet, about the wedding day. But I imagined it must have been a happy occasion. *Aren't they all?* I imagined she must have dressed in white, with a high hairdo and wild curls, placed deliberately by a stylist that her father would have brought in especially for the day. Of all the women I'd met, I couldn't think of one who would have looked more the part than Erica.

Although the woman pictured and fixed inside the pages was beautiful, too.

'Even though you're not Erica...'

I turned another page, saw another snapshot of a woman wearing white. The fabric looked similar to the slip of lace I'd pulled from the box already. But how can you tell one white from another? I wasn't well-versed enough in wedding wear. Instead, I skimmed another page and saw the woman surrounded by equally beautiful women wearing a series of dresses; the designs were all different but the burst of emerald green the same for each. They were a chorus of laughter in one image, the portrait of innocence with close-lipped smiles in the next. It took me three turns to find anyone else – the father and mother of the bride, I guessed – then another two to find the man himself.

He was young, handsome, happy. The suit he wore was an ill fit for his body shape but still he wore it well. Like his bride, there were pictures of him surrounded by laughing women, but also men; one with the bridesmaids, another with groomsmen. They had the shared demeanour of a friendship group that knew they were attractive; I recognised their postures, the self-confidence of twenty-something men in the presence of beautiful women. I only guessed at their ages, though bride and groom both looked like they were from the same bracket. Although neither of them looked old enough to be getting married. I turned the page and thought: *Though that probably says more about me.* The proximity to the commitment made my stomach turn over. Though the next time my stomach turned, it was for a different reason altogether.

I didn't recognise the handwriting. From the angle the photograph had been taken, though, I could recognise something of the man's smile. I realised then that I hadn't seen too many pictures away from this scrapbook, to give me a point of comparison. There were occasional photographs in the biographies I had stashed away at home, although most pictures there were of Erica; hardly ever him. Still, there was something in the upturn of his mouth; the way he looked at the camera like he might seduce its holder. Then, there, underneath the photograph of them signing the register, it read:

Mrs Roger Miller.

It was written in three different scripts. I imagined the bride signing her name, practising the new signature that she would carry for the rest of her life. *Only she didn't.* The husband, I realised, was definitely Roger. Roger, captured years before any other pictures I had seen of him. Roger, with a First Wife who hadn't been mentioned. Roger, married to someone who wasn't Erica...

There was a commotion upstairs. I imagined Erica knocking something from a side table, throwing herself awake; rushing down the stairs and catching me in the act of– *What do I think I'm doing?* I hit the camera icon on my phone and snapped picture after picture without knowing what I was capturing. But I turned the pages, replaced the items, and documented each step like it might mean something to my future self. I resisted the urge to snatch the garter away with me. This wasn't the time for pocketing murderabilia. When the box was reassembled, I rushed out and closed the door. Rather than wait for the offensive then, I moved to defence. I hadn't heard her bedroom door open, so I climbed the stairs towards it. I knocked once, twice, and when I didn't hear either an invite or a dismissal, I decided she mightn't be able to hear me over the struggled sounds still coming from inside. She was coughing in a way that I recognised from when she'd been sitting still for too long.

The door's hinges announced my arrival. I waited for her to acknowledge me but, when she didn't manage a greeting, I spoke plainly. 'You're sick.' Still, there was nothing. She stared at the ceiling as though I weren't there and I wondered whether it was wishful thinking. 'Should I go back downstairs and pretend I haven't noticed?'

There was a long pause before she said, 'Stage four.' Another delay, then, 'Aggressive.'

# CHAPTER TWENTY-TWO

What's another word for morbid?

It was a friends' night in, and Raf's turn to host. He was notoriously terrible at the job, though, so ahead of time we all agreed on our separate snack and drink duties. I bumped into Rita and Annie in the hallway of Raf's building. I was holding two share buckets of popcorn that I'd collected on the way; meanwhile they were juggling seven bottles of wine between them. There were going to be five of us altogether; a little wine didn't go a long way with those numbers. The three of us said our hellos and shared our kisses on cheeks, then trod the rest of the way to Raf's front door together. Rita and Annie swapped war stories about their respective days at work, but I stayed solemnly quiet about my own day.

I'd spent the afternoon in Erica's garden while she dipped in and out of narratives: about the cancer; about her father; occasionally she spoke of Roger. The sessions had lacked focus since she'd confided in me about her being ill. For me, spending my days with an accused murderess had been sinister enough to begin with. But knowing the motivations behind the project had made me lose our way. I found I ricocheted between trusting and not trusting Erica; feeling close, only to soon feel the opposite. The case of The Missing Wife, added to The Missing Best Friend, hadn't helped me to ease into the work either. While my days away from Erica were meant to be spent typing, filing, organising my notes, instead I found I was spending more and more time looking for breadcrumbs of the missing women in her wake. *Is this all worth it?* I asked myself, not for the first time, while Rita explained what was fundamentally wrong with her corner of the fashion industry.

'So, why do you work in it?' Annie snapped.

'Ladies.' Raf pulled the door open and pressed pause on their growing argument. From behind him there rose the sound of disgruntled voices. He rolled his eyes. 'Come, join the argument.'

'Oh, good. What are we arguing over in here?' I handed over the popcorn while Rita and Annie knocked bottles further down the corridor in front of us.

'The new Erica Miller documentary came out today. The boys are arguing about–'

'How guilty she is!' Luke interrupted.

'Which she isn't,' Max added.

'Bitch fight.' Rita cracked the seal on a bottle of wine. 'Anyone?'

'I'll take a red.' I was the first to answer. Glugging wine like it was squash would at least keep me out of the group discussion.

'In the red corner we have Max, ding, ding,' Annie said as she passed him a glass of wine. 'And in the blue corner with Luke, ding, ding. Raf, pick a side.'

'Christ, I don't know. I find it *slightly* suspect that his killer has never been found.'

'That's because she was found.' Luke sipped his drink. 'And tried, and let off.'

'How many people get away with murder, like, actually?' Max snapped back.

Luke snorted. 'How the fuck is anyone expected to answer that question with a degree of accuracy? You're reaching. As far as we know, people get away with murder every day.' He started to shout statistics about serial killers in America, detection time, famous British names...

'We get it,' Rita said flatly, 'you're morbid.'

'I'm not morbid, I'm just well informed.'

'Okay, smart arse, if you're so well informed,' Max followed in behind Raf, to make a human shield of our host, 'if Erica Miller *did* do away with her husband, then why haven't they managed to try her for it second a time around?'

Annie raised a hand. 'I know this one.' Luke waved her permission to take the floor. 'It's a little-known fact that UK law actually has a double jeopardy policy.'

Something tensed in my gut.

'Without *considerable* evidence, there can't be grounds to try a person twice over for the same crime. Considerable evidence being something physical that wasn't picked up the first time around as part of the case. Or a confession.' She paused to take a hurried swig of her wine. 'I would guess a confession would do the trick, too.'

Luke high-fived her. 'What she said.'

'Hey,' I nudged Annie, 'that's true?'

'One hundred per cent. So unless the case is still open, somewhere, with one detective or another squirrelling away evidence, then they're unlikely to find anything worthwhile. Unless Erica Miller ups and drops a confession on their plates.'

'Which would be hard for her to do,' Luke added his two pence, 'given that no one has been able to track the woman down for years.'

White noise rushed in through each ear and I missed the

immediate responses. Did it matter that double jeopardy existed? I wasn't altogether sure. But this new information felt significant. I pressed it between tissue paper and stashed it in my back pocket, along with every other hypothetical thing that I didn't yet know about Erica; what she had or hadn't done. I didn't know enough about the original evidence yet either; other than it was circumstantial enough not to matter when it came to a conviction. If the manuscript I was now working on was going to unearth more, though, I needed to be prepared.

*Why?* I tried to cut the worries off. *In case she really does up and confess?*

'You two are the most annoying double act. Did I tell you that?' Max said but his stare was fixed on the paused opening credits of the documentary. It didn't sound like I'd missed anything major when I tuned back in. 'Annoying and macabre.'

'Well informed,' Luke corrected him.

'Do we really have to watch this?' I asked when the conversation finally lulled.

Raf was the first to look my way. 'Not feeling it?'

*I can't think of anything worse.*

I shook my head. I couldn't admit such a strong reaction against watching the feature though. Because what would I follow it up with: the fact that I *do* know where Erica Miller is? The fact that I'd pulled into her driveaway not twelve hours ago; sipped her lemonade, enjoyed the afternoon shade of her garden? Christ, even confess that I'd offered to drive her to a doctor's appointment in a week's time? She'd refused, thank God, because the offer slipped out by mistake. Still, I threw down another mouthful of wine and let the acid burn through the beginnings of my honest answer. Instead I suggested, 'God, it's just a bit grim, isn't it?'

'Grim is what they said about her in the media before the trial started,' Luke answered.

Rita hit his upper arm. 'Why do you know so much about this?'

'I worked on a prison exposé a couple of years ago.' Luke was a freelance journalist, and a bloody good one at that. He loved the thrill of the chase that came with outing a liar, or shaming someone; he'd always enjoyed that, too. 'There were rumours flung about that the rich and famous got special treatment in the clink so I looked a little into the wealth divide. Interesting stuff.'

'Can we just get this over with?' Max asked with the same disinterest I felt.

Raf hit play. 'Let's.'

Roger's first wife was called Hannah Wilcox. They married right out of school, only to spend their blissful years arguing about the tribulations of real life. Then, Roger met Erica. He upped and left Hannah in favour of a new woman who would offer him a better standard of living.

'And a better style of death, no doubt,' Luke mumbled from behind his phone. Rita shushed him and slapped his arm again for emphasis. But there wasn't much more information about the first wife after that. Either she hadn't been available to comment or she hadn't made a comment worth including. The most they managed was to show pictures, but there was nothing of hers and Roger's wedding. *Because the evidence is all locked in Erica's box room,* I guessed. Though they showed pictures of Hannah and Roger together from school, likely pulled from their alumni database – or old friends looking to make a quick pound.

There was an easy fade in and out montage of Hannah and Roger, smiling and laughing and drunk on love. They had those stupid-happy expressions that come with the first throes of affection. I'd seen some of it in their wedding photographs, too. But what also struck me, as the final photograph faded to black and the interval played, was how similar Hannah looked to Erica's own Ruby. Their complexions and hair colour were both the same, and their smiles both upturned more so on one side, giving full-face pictures something especially endearing. Although their builds were different, anyone who paired them together would spot the similarities still. *Did Roger and Erica have a type?* I wondered. *Did they like their missing women to look a certain way?*

'Prue,' Annie tapped my forearm, 'are you with me?'

'Christ, sorry.' I fumbled for my phone. 'I just remembered something for work and I was miles away. What did you say?'

'I asked if you wanted more wine.'

I put my hand over my glass. 'No, I think I'm okay, thanks.'

'Juice? A carbonated sugar kick of your choosing?' Raf, ever the host. 'Ice water?'

'I mean, you could get Max to stop bogarting that popcorn I brought.'

'I'm stress eating.' He spoke around a mouthful of corn. 'Aren't you stressed?'

'Max, lemme ask,' Luke leaned around Rita to get a good look at Max's face, 'are you stressed out watching this because you're starting to think she's guilty?'

*Maybe.* While they argued out the basics of Erica's for and against verdict, I unlocked my phone and thumbed into the notes application. Before this, I hadn't been able to find out a full name for Roger's first wife. Maybe the documentarians hadn't been able to find her, but I reasoned it was at least worth a look; if only to set my mind at ease. *Or pour gasoline on the flames of it.*

'Detective Inspector Fowler is interviewed as part of this, you know, lads. Why don't we save the Vaseline wrestling until he's had a chance to speak?' Raf added as he wandered back into the debates, a glass of wine in one hand and water in the other.

He handed me the latter. 'You look a little peaky, honey. Make sure you're hydrated, okay?'

I smiled. 'Thank you.'

Annie clicked her fingers and stared into the ceiling. 'Remind me who Fowler is?'

'Arresting officer.' Again, Max's response came with a spray of corn.

'You're going to burst kernels all over my living room.'

'Raf, some things are more important than soft furnishings.'

'Bitch, you take that back.'

A soft humour moved through the group then, allowing a reprieve from the tension and suspicion that had sat among us for the evening. Even so, I still added Fowler's name to the note on my phone and sat with a lead weight in my belly while we listened to his dealings with Erica. He relayed how he'd felt something off about her the first time they met – 'You know when you can't get a read on someone?' – and how his suspicions grew as the case advanced – 'I could never quite set my ideas on her to one side long enough to entertain someone else, not really. People thought I was blinkered, but...' They interviewed Fowler three times, according to the narration, and they picked the perfect soundbite for his exit.

'So, to be clear, you firmly believed that Erica Miller killed Roger Miller?'

He shook his head. 'Present tense, kid. I firmly *believe* it.'

CHAPTER TWENTY-THREE

W hat's the collective noun for missing women?

Hannah was as difficult to find as Ruby. But I lived in hope that there must be some trace of her. I wasn't sure whether she would have reverted to her maiden name or not after the divorce, though, which meant that for every search that involved Hannah Wilcox, I looked under a stone for Hannah Miller. When asked, Erica had been honest enough about not knowing Hannah existed. But she hadn't given me anywhere near enough information to track the woman down outside of our meetings. *Because you're not meant to be doing it...* I thought as I clicked into another directory. Social media had been my starting point because it always was these days. But neither version of Hannah's name was distinct enough to throw up a small amount of search results; there were hundreds of them both. And even though I'd seen the woman through her teenage years and into her early twenties, that didn't help much when it came to imagining how she might look now.

It was eleven in the evening on an Erica day when a proverbial light bulb snapped on.

I pulled up a search engine and keyed in the name of the

documentary. The directors were both transparent, their personal websites high on the list of search results. *So they know their way around SEO*, which I hoped would mean they might know their way around tracking down people via the net a little better than I could boast. I clicked to the website of the man – Yusuf – first and skipped over the preamble of About Me in favour of going straight to Contact:

> Hi there. I'm doing some research into the Erica Miller case and I'd really appreciate the help of an expert. Might you be able to spare a second or two to discuss some of your findings? I'd really appreciate it. Thanks for your time and I hope to hear from you. Best. Prue.

Like a true unprofessional, I copied the message into Director Two's contact form on her website and sent exactly the same query to Rebecca. But at least no one could say I wasn't consistent.

There were so many tabs open, so many frantic notes and crossed-through post-its; spine-cracked books and A4 pads, each devoted to a different avenue of research. I had arrived at a point of not knowing whether I was plotting a book for Erica, or against her. *Could it be both?* I pushed myself away from my desk and trod to the kitchen. The living room looked like a crime scene and the irony wasn't lost. But the kitchen was a haven still. I flicked the kettle to boil and grabbed coffee granules from a nearby cupboard. While the water clicked and hummed to heat, I pulled leftover pizza from the fridge and inhaled a cold slice in three bites. I couldn't remember when I'd last eaten.

I took coffee and another two slices back to the living room with me; pizza in one hand, cup in the other, and a corner of one triangle already in my mouth. I'd reverted to student, and I still didn't know what my final piece of work would show evidence of. But at least I wasn't the only one working late into the evening. Yusuf had already replied, eight minutes after my own message had arrived with him:

Hi Prue. It's a really interesting case. I'd love to talk about it some more. We could get Becky involved too depending on your interests, although she is on holiday right now. Still, let's talk at a suitable time. My details are...

I keyed in his number and checked the clock in the corner of my screen: 11.23pm. *Is* now *a suitable time?* While my thumb hovered over the call button I went back and forth on the question. He'd replied, after all. I decided, too, that if a disgruntled man answered then I could always hang up and plead coincidence, and before I'd even allowed for the opportunity of talking myself out of it the phone was to my ear and–

'Yusuf speaking.'

*Not disgruntled.* 'Hi there, Yusuf. It's Prue Carr here, I literally just contacted you thro–'

'Wow, you aren't wasting much time,' he said but there was a smile cracking through the words. 'Good to hear from a fellow murder buff.' He laughed, then, and I tried to but, *Christ, murder buff?* 'The Erica Miller doc was a really interesting one actually. Becky and I have had *a lot* of mixed feedback about the whole thing. Hey, you're not secretly getting in touch to rant and rave about the woman's innocence, are you?' There was still an audible smile there. But if he was asking, I thought he must have had plenty of complaints.

'You've had a lot of people do that?'

'Maybe not a lot, but certainly a few.'

'Because people think she's innocent?'

'Hey,' he half-laughed and it sounded like his enthusiasm for this line of enquiry was already wilting, 'everyone has an opinion about what she did, right? Which side of the fence are you on?'

'I'm open-minded.' I'd been ready with the answer. 'But I'm actually more interested in Hannah Wilcox than I am about–'

'Oh, Hannah? She definitely thinks Erica did it.' His huffs and laughs were already grating on me. It must have been murder to work with him. 'That's why she didn't want to be front facing on the film, you know? She said she was happy to talk with us and all but she didn't want to be... Christ, how did she phrase it? Visible, I think that's the word she used.'

It spoke at a volume that my gut reaction was this: *So, she is alive.*

'You actually spoke to Hannah?'

'We did. Paid her a visit. Obviously I can't say where. Do you know, it's hats off to Becky for that one because I lost my shit *very* early on with trying to find that woman. She really didn't make it easy. But Becky is pretty well connected and she managed to track her down, approached her with caution, made all the right noises.' He was joking again, but I couldn't help but wonder how scared the woman must have been to want so much careful wrapping around her involvement with the documentary. 'Her main concern was whether we'd keep her face hidden or not. It's been a long time since those photographs were taken and all; she looks fairly different now. Hey, don't we all with time?'

*So she'd given them the photographs?*

'Look, I know this is unlikely,' I started, with a turn of nerves, 'but Hannah's where–'

'No can do,' he answered before I'd got there. 'I just can't.'

I sighed. 'I was pushing my luck.'

'Hey, a little, but you have to in this game. It isn't even about hogging the sources, though, you know, it's just about protecting them. Hannah doesn't know where Erica is. She'd like it kept that Erica doesn't know where she is either. Fair is fair and all that.'

'Completely.' I finished scribbling what I'd been able to snatch. 'Becky, your colleague, that is? She must have worked pretty damn hard to find her though.' I thought I'd try one last tactic. After all, sometimes you could shake a tree's fruit loose from kicking a different spot on the bark. 'I looked through high heavens for a Wilcox and a Miller and I couldn't find her anywhere.'

'Oh, Prue, I can tell you this much...' *Bingo.* I had my pen ready. 'She isn't either.'

'Wait, she changed her name?'

He murmured agreement. 'Hannah Wilcox, Hannah Miller. She doesn't exist.'

---

When I woke up the following morning, the living room was dotted with half-arsed ideas. Some of them scribbled in thick black writing on A4 sheets, others in small script to get them squeezed onto the back of a receipt. Whatever had been close enough to write on, I'd grabbed it. Now, the only thing within reach was my phone which was humming a ringtone that belonged to none other than–

'Connie, what do you want?'

'I'm outside your building.' There was a heavy pause. 'I think your buzzer is broken.'

I trod down to let her in and found her loitering outside with a bouncing baby boy on her hip. I wasn't an especially maternal woman. Having been around Connie's offspring intermittently hadn't made a difference in that. In fact, in true caring sister fashion, Connie had even offered to make me godmother to this particular child – Scotty, to be Scott when he matured – and I'd been so thrown by the suggestion that I'd actually laughed. Scott(y) and I had patched up since then; I gave him a kiss on the cheek and he giggled as I saw them into the building. But I wasn't sure Connie had ever really let it go.

'Is everything okay?'

She led the way to my own front door and pushed it open. 'You tell me.'

*Fuck. What occasion have I missed?* 'It isn't this one's birthday, is it?'

'No it isn't *this one's* birth...' Connie petered out when she walked into my living room. 'Prue, what the hell is going on in here? It looks like your laptop exploded.' I fell over myself to hide the evidence of Erica. 'Or your brain.'

'I'm sorry, I was working late and– Sorry, let me just.' I quickly closed the tabbed books showing Erica's face in various stages of criminality. 'There you go. Now, tea?'

'Sit.'

Even though it was my house – and Connie the younger sister – I still did as I was told. Scotty gave me a little smile, as though he, too, could see that my decision-making was bang on. I gave him a wink in return and he giggled again. *It can't be this easy to have a kid*, I thought, *look at how tired Connie is from it.* My sister – the beauty to my brains – was heavy around the eyes. I wondered how well Scotty was sleeping.

'Con, are you sure everything's okay?'

'Prue, do you know that you've screened like, five phone calls from me?' I opened my mouth to answer; to deny the allegation. 'Maybe even more, actually, if you check your missed call log. What is going on with you late–'

The ringtone that I'd assigned to Erica cut through Connie's monologue. I tried my best not to react but, *What fucking timing you have, Erica,* I thought as I scratched at my forehead and looked around the room like I was a visitor in the space. For a second I entertained the idea that I might feign not hearing the phone at all but Connie's raised eyebrow soon put the stop on that idea. I reached across to grab the handset from the coffee table and checked the screen, despite knowing the sound all too well.

'You have to be kidding me.'

My thumb was over the answer button. 'It's work.'

'Well, this is family.'

*I know an ultimatum when I hear one.* I put the phone down. 'It'll go to voicemail.'

Two minutes later, the clunk of a voicemail message interrupted Connie's soliloquy on self-care and family values and – *I hope Erica is okay.* There were a few other things from Connie. But nothing to do with work – or Erica.

# CHAPTER TWENTY-FOUR

What's the word for falsifying an alibi?

When Erica turned around there was a butter knife in her hand, and a smile on her face that would have been flirtatious under other circumstances. 'Now, *I* didn't lie to the police.' It was semantics. But I didn't say so. Besides which, Erica had a way of saying things so plainly that I sometimes felt unreasonable for finding fault with whatever she'd said. 'Come on, Prue, have you ever tried to talk a parent out of something? They're impossible to deal with when they've set their minds and my father was no different to the rest of them. He just wanted...' She fizzled out.

'To protect you,' I completed the sentence.

'Yes.' She nodded and I saw her jaw shift as though she were chewing over the word. 'That's exactly what he wanted, all his life. Anyway, you live alone, don't you?'

I wasn't sure it was information I wanted to admit. 'I'm not sure I see...'

'Hypothetically, you live alone. Imagine, then, that on any given night of the week you're at home, alone. How would you prove that to someone?'

*There must be an answer.* I desperately wanted there to be an answer, but, 'I don't know.'

She shrugged. 'Think on it then. While you're thinking on it, grab a fresh bottle from the fridge, will you? If you're staying over, the pair of us should at least make the most of having an alibi apiece for the evening.'

I followed instructions. I ate and drank and tried to remain merry. I even slurred my words appropriately through to bedtime. I had a friendship circle that had long ago established a high tolerance for alcohol in me though. Between that and the bowl of pasta at dinner, I was confident I was nowhere near the level of tipsy Erica wanted me to be. But I thought she might be freer with the truth if she thought I was less likely to remember it the following morning. She topped up my drink at regular intervals, initiated a new bottle, offered me a cigarette even: 'Come on, you won't let a woman smoke alone?' I'd taken the bait and bit down on the filter while she lit the loose tobacco end. The evening became uncomfortably intimate too quickly and the glow of wine in my belly pushed and shoved me between the rock of wanting the closeness and the hard place of knowing how dangerous it was. Erica wobbled when she stood from the seat outside and I wondered whether it was the alcohol or the medication. Still, like a gracious host, she held out a hand for me and suggested that we call time on whatever it was we were doing.

'You look like you need a good night's sleep.'

I nodded my agreement and took the offered hand, all the while thinking, *But I could rinse you for information until the small hours.* I knew better than to bite the hand that was feeding me leads, though, and if Erica were suggesting we call it a night it was because her beans were spilled enough for one sitting. On the walk from garden to stairs to spare bedroom, she kept a hand on or near my waist and my breath caught whenever her fingers tightened a fraction.

The spare room was pristine. It could have been pulled from the pages of a magazine spread. The bed was covered in strategically placed cushions, and a brushed cotton throw across the bottom of the steel-grey duvet. The curtains were drawn already, with neat folds running down them in a way that interrupted their geometric design. From my first scan of the space, I came to expect a mint on the pillow and a menu form on the bedside.

'Do you have guests often?' I turned from my standpoint in the centre of the room. She was leaning in the doorway, and for the first time I noticed that her eyes looked tipsy-tired. 'The place looks like it's been ready and waiting.'

She shrugged. 'You never know.'

There was a long pause, then, while I looked around the room again. When I glanced back at Erica, I realised she'd been watching me. She leaned into the room to grab at the door handle.

'I'll be seeing you in the morning,' she said, although it sounded like she was asking.

'Thank you, Erica. Goodnight.'

I waited for the click of the door, and the sound of her treading away. There was moonlight creeping through a crack in the curtains, but I left it. I wanted to keep an eye on the shape of the room. Soon, I lay down on top of the covers, still in my clothes, and counted conspiracy theories until I fell asleep.

The morning after, we greeted each other like old friends. I made a show of apologising, as though embarrassed for my (faux) slurred words the night before. Erica brushed it away though – 'It was the most fun I've had in a long time.' – and I felt reassured that she'd believed the put-on. She suggested breakfast, too, as a cure-all for the hangovers that neither of us looked to truly have, and I agreed. She'd let slip a confession the evening before, with her father's alibi, and I wondered whether the fresh country air would loosen anything else.

I waited dotingly for her at the end of the driveway while she locked up the house. When she joined me, we started the walk alongside each other. I dug my hands deep into my pockets and unlocked my phone; it was already set to record. And it was worth it for the information that came. Like tumbling leaves from an old bark, Erica shed one truth after another – 'Dad's credit card was stolen.' – which included details that weren't true at all. 'Roger and I had an argument and I called my father for an ear,' she said as we rounded the bend, bringing the village into sight. The timer was on, I realised then, so I played a brazen card.

'What evidence did they actually have *against* you?'

I knew, of course. Or I knew a watercolour outline; things reported in second-hand sources. But I wanted the real thing – on tape.

Erica laughed, clicked her fingers and made a whooshing sound. 'Nothing that didn't disappear, just like that.' She set a hand on my arm then, to stop me from walking. 'Prue, you aren't writing anything down.'

I forced a laugh. 'I have a feeling I'll remember.'

She murmured in agreement. 'I suppose that's fair. I know I must be a little...' She stuck out her tongue, crossed her eyes and circled a finger next to her forehead. She reminded me of the crazy-eyed emoji and my laugh was a genuine one then. 'Speaking of crazy, maybe I can ask my own question of you? Especially now we're spitting distance from a cooked breakfast.'

'Christ,' I rubbed my stomach, 'I am genuinely starving.'

'That'll be the walk.' She stopped us then. 'So, my turn?' I nodded agreement and kept a hand on my stomach; *it might be nerves not hunger.* 'Now that you know so much about me, why don't you tell me why it is that you're taking fluoxetine?'

There was static between my ears. 'I'm sorry?' Even my own voice sounded distorted, underwater somehow. 'How do you...' I tried again but I couldn't hear over my panic.

'Last night.' She reached for my forearm and squeezed, softly. 'Prue, don't look so worried. There's really nothing to be embarrassed or awkward about–'

'No, I...' I tried to shake away shadows of worry that were clinging on. 'I don't remember even telling you that, though, when did I...' I tried to laugh; a nervous laugh if nothing else. Because Erica looked fine with the conversation that we were having. Whereas I imagined I must look– *Like I'm shitting myself*, I thought, *because that's certainly a bit how it feels.* 'God, how drunk *was* I?'

She shrugged. 'It was only small talk.'

*When*, I wanted to push, *when, from our evening together, are you going to try to convince me that I told you this?*

'Roger was on something similar for a time,' she said, as she started walking again. I was glad not to have to look at her head-on anymore. 'There was a period in his life when he was deeply sad about nothing at all and they started him on... God, I don't know, some godforsaken tablet or another. They do it for everyone now, don't they?' We came to a stop outside the pub. I shielded my eyes from the glare of brilliant white clouds and looked up, as though assessing the weather. I still wasn't ready to look at Erica; again, I worried about turning to stone. 'I don't mean that disrespectfully, of course. If you need them, you need them.'

I pulled in a big breath before I met her stare. 'Roger needed them?'

She nodded. 'I think Roger always needed something in life that he wasn't getting.'

I couldn't decide whether she sounded sad or bitter.

'Well, I can't talk mental health on an empty stomach. Are we in or out?'

'Out? I'll order for us both.' Not for the first time, then, I felt like a trophy to Erica. I could sit outside, look pretty, be taken care of. I wondered whether that was what she wanted. The thought wrapped around me like an old knit blanket; the kind that brings with it an itch you can never reach. 'Full English? I'll get tea and orange juice. It'll help your head.'

'You sound like you're well-versed in all this.'

She laughed. 'I haven't always been a bore. Besides, I know how to take care of people. This is another thing you have in common with Roger.'

I didn't like the comparison but I didn't have time to protest. When she'd disappeared into the pub, I picked a table in the shade and pulled out my phone. I sighed in relief at the sight of the ticking clock face; it had recorded the full walk from Erica's to here. But I ended the function, then, and pulled up a fresh iMessage instead: "Need help with a case. Will pay in coffee. Free soon?" I waited until the pop-up showed the message had delivered before I put the handset away. Elbows on table, I cradled my chin and watched the world move. And I recited possible lies like they were grounding exercises: *One: I have anxiety.* There were people busying about as though this was an entirely normal day. *Two: I'm depressed. Isn't everyone these days?* It was like no one else knew that my privacy had been invaded; no one knew that Erica knew more about me than she should. *Three: What fucking business is it of yours to know anyway?* I could have leapt up and across the stretch of small car park in front, grabbed anyone and explained that–

'Prue?'

I shook the thoughts away. 'God, sorry, world of my own.'

'It looked that way.' Erica sat down and pushed a glass of

orange juice toward my side of the table. 'The countryside must have that sort of impact on you, when you're so accustomed to the inner-city. It's a shame, really, that when you live here you get so used to the space.'

*Why is she making us have a normal conversation?* But no sooner had I thought it and...

'Anyway, you were about to tell me why you're depressed.' She smiled a wide and terrifying grin like a children's book character that might eat me whole.

*No,* I thought, *I wasn't.* But she'd gifted me the start of a lie, so I told her the end of it.

CHAPTER TWENTY-FIVE

What's a better word for financially liable?

Lola and I went way back – to the days when she was a lowly IT assistant at a firm I did content writing for at university. We'd had a brief fling that didn't quite ignite. But the embers had carried a steady friendship over the years, and I knew her well enough to call in a favour. She'd replied to my offer of coffee telling me to name a day, so I had. I picked a time when I was an hour away from meeting my sister and her pet project of a husband. I was anxious enough about seeing them; the last thing I needed was to carry my anxieties for Erica along with me. Meeting Lola at least helped me to feel like I was doing something. So I'd chosen the day and date, and I asked Lola to pick a place that was convenient to her. Her preference was an internet café in the centre of town.

'It smells like sweat in here.' I leaned over the table to kiss her cheek.

'Does it?' She looked around. 'Honestly, I hardly even notice these things anymore. They've claimed me as one of their own.'

Lola worked as a freelance hacker now. But if anyone asked

she was still the same lowly IT assistant she'd always been. She'd been my go-to for work advice over the years, though, and there were times when even my friends had relied on her for their projects, too. She was a shared resource – and a woman who could definitely be trusted.

'You're looking good, Carr.'

'You don't look so bad yourself.'

'So…'

I laughed. 'Straight to it?'

'I'm a busy woman.' She looked at her watch. 'Plus, I've got another client meeting me here in less than half an hour and I wouldn't want you to cross paths.'

The mention of a client made my stomach clench. *Does Erica have a Lola?* 'Your clients, how do you meet them, if you don't mind me asking?'

She arched an eyebrow. 'I do mind. I pride myself on privacy.'

'Well, if that isn't irony then–'

'My own privacy, that is,' she interrupted me and flashed a tight smile. 'I don't give a shit about other people's.'

Despite my history with Lola, I felt a flare of dislike for her then. I was on the right side of her, which kept me safe. But there was another Lola out there, one that Erica might be having coffee with at some secluded city centre spot; one who was rifling through the innards of my life for a handsome sum and–

Lola snapped her fingers in front of my face. 'Drifting?'

'Thinking. Sorry.' I leaned in and lowered my voice. 'How easy do you think I would be to hack?'

'Do you want me to show you?' she asked. I recoiled at the suggestion and she laughed; a teeth-bearing laugh that made me feel small and worried. 'Wow, you really don't want me to show you. Okay. Prue, I'm going into the basics of this because you don't care.' She paused, shook her head, and revised, 'Or maybe you won't understand. Either way, anyone can be hacked.' She paused to think and revise. 'Most people can be hacked. You aren't a computer whizz. You're more careful than the average person but you also need *everyone* around you to be that careful, too, so...'

'What do you mean, sorry? People can get to my stuff through other people?'

'Ish? I more mean, your personal documents might be safe on your personal devices. But you can't be sure that the gym you use won't get hacked for your address. Or the work system you use won't get hacked for your calendar. Do you see?'

I sucked in a big breath. 'Or my doctors won't get hacked?'

'Sure.' She was looking behind me. I wondered whether her next client was early. In a rapid and unsettling montage, I imagined Lola's client as Erica: me turning; her eyes stretching; Lola standing; Erica saying...

'Doctors are generally quite safe in terms of their systems, though, I mean, they *have* to be with all the shit they store.' Lola pulled me back into the room. 'But sure, there's no reason why someone tech-savvy enough couldn't do it. Although it might be easier just to bribe a receptionist at the doctor's surgery to give up someone's medical records.' She sipped her drink and met my gaze then. 'Is it anyone I can help with?'

*Me*, I thought, although I didn't want to say it. Erica had found out about the medication somehow. And despite my best efforts at raking over the evening with her, I couldn't find a black space big enough for missing information – nor could I fathom why my prescription would even have come up in polite chit-chat, even if I had been drunk. *Which I wasn't*, I reassured myself again.

'What if I didn't want to hack someone?' I asked. 'What if I wanted to find out whether someone had been hacked?'

She narrowed her eyes. 'People usually know. Money is missing, information is leaked–'

'It's nothing as groundbreaking as that. I'm not talking public, make-a-splash information. I'm talking personal, private records. It's nothing worth leaking to the press.' I forced a laugh. I could hear an edge of panic creeping in. But Lola already looked bored with what I'd brought her. 'Maybe its only value is to get close to someone. To make it seem like you know them better than you do.'

Lola only shook her head, though, then checked her watch. 'Frankly, why bother?'

There was a really long pause before I asked, 'Don't you ever feel bad?'

'No,' she answered – with no pause at all. 'It's a living. And my client is here early.'

A heavy breath fell out of me when I turned round and saw a middle-aged man loitering at the order point. He shifted from one foot to the other while waiting, as though unsure of what to do with himself. He didn't belong in a place like this. But then, neither did I. Lola looked right at home, though, as she rifled through her laptop bag, then pulled out a wad of notes and set them on the table. She raised her eyebrows at the pile.

'It's so much worse than he expects it to be,' she said, staring at the papers.

'Well,' I stood, 'in that case I should let you get started.' I tugged my bag onto my shoulder and hovered for a second too long, unsure of whether to lean in for a second kiss. 'Thank you, Lola, for filling in some blanks.'

'Any time.' She waved the man over. 'But you actually didn't buy me a coffee so...'

'Next time?'

She nodded. 'I'll go ahead and put something in your calendar.'

It was a joke. I knew it was a joke. Yet, I couldn't shake the weight of it. So I left to meet Connie with the same ball of anxiety I'd started with. If anything, the walk from Point A to Point B gave my mind too much roaming space to add further worries. I was actually relieved when I looped through a side street and came out on a different side of the city, to face a different blaze that needed to be doused…

I didn't often see Connie and Robert together. 'Call me Bert, why don't you?' he asked every time. But I was bankrolling his gambling so I reasoned I could call him whatever I fucking wanted. The two of them sat across from me in a Wetherspoons; it was their idea of taking me for a thank-you meal. But while we browsed our respective menus, I wondered whether it was a we-need-a-favour meal, too. It was strange to see them both without the kids in tow, too, and I found that when they weren't around I was even less inclined to do Robert any favours. *So maybe I do have a maternal instinct*, it occurred to me, then, for my little sister and the beautiful mistakes that had come from her dalliance with this waster who had knocked her up – twice.

'Prue,' he started, in a voice like toffee sauce; nice on the surface but likely to erode you. 'What is it that you fancy?'

I looked from him to her and back again. 'That's it? There's no more?'

Connie cracked a smile although I thought she looked nervous. 'It's just dinner.'

'You've been really good to me and Con. We just wanted…' He reached a hand out for hers and she obliged; I paid close attention to how hard he squeezed. 'We just wanted to say thank you for everything, that's all, and to tell you that,' he squeezed again, 'I'm really trying this time. Aren't I, Con?'

'He really is.'

*This time.* I wondered whether that was an admission of having not *really* tried before. 'Going to meetings?'

'Meetings and everything.'

I was glad to hear it, given that it was a condition of my lending him money at all. But he'd never been able to stick to the meetings; he was too drawn, instead, to the sparkly lights and the clink of money and the sound of his children crying with hunger because my sister couldn't afford a full food shop that week.

I sucked in the insults. 'Good, Robert, that's really good.'

'Bertie.'

'What are you having, Connie?' I asked, as though I hadn't heard.

'Scampi, chips, no peas.'

I laughed. She'd picked our childhood favourite. 'I'll have the same.' I dropped my menu on the table. 'Robert?' I flashed him a tight smile, then; a dare. 'What are you having?'

He passed his menu to Connie but kept his stare fixed on me. 'Surprise me, babe.'

'Oh, I'm going to order then, am I?' Her tone was playful. She looked less tired than when I'd last seen her, and I was relieved at that at least. I kept an eye on her until she'd wiggled into a small spot at the bar, wedged between two clusters of men who looked like they'd been drinking since yesterday. She was out of earshot, though, and Robert must have checked that, too, before he started.

'Connie says you're working on a new book.'

'Mm, have been for a while.'

'Suppose you can't tell us about it.' He laughed. 'Top secret?'

'I'm non-disclosured into a corner.'

'Must be a lot of money in those bigger projects though.'

I looked at him for the first time then. 'Enough to support myself and a family.'

'Ouch.' He leaned back and widened the gap between us. 'Shots fired.'

'Oh, come on. You're asking me about work?'

'I'm interested.'

'Yeah, in my monthly take-home.'

'Prue, come on, can't we–'

'No.' He looked as though I'd slapped him. I wondered whether my sister had ever flat out refused a request without hearing it in full. *It'll do you a favour to hear it from someone, either way.* 'Whatever the end of that is, no. Make no mistake,' I leaned over the table, encroached over to his side, 'if it weren't for my sister, you and I would be nothing to each other. I love her, so I tolerate you, and I actually give a shit about your kids eating a proper meal each night.'

There was a long and uncomfortable silence while I checked my phone – mostly for something to do. Stunned, Robert waited until I stashed the handset away before he spoke.

'I was only asking about the bloody book.'

'Oh, no point asking about that,' Connie said, catching the wrong tone of the conversation. 'It's top-secret sneaky crime writing that Prue won't say anything about.'

'What?' I snapped.

'Crime writing, eh?' Robert latched on. He whistled. 'Hope you don't get stabbed.'

Connie slapped his arm. 'Christ, what a thing to even think.'

He and I locked eyes and I cocked an eyebrow. 'Yeah, Robert, what a thing.'

'Anyway, she isn't researching *crime*, she's researching *criminals*,' Connie added.

'Why do you know so much about this?' I asked, and she laughed.

'I mean, I don't. Not really. Food should be about half an hour.'

'Plenty of time to talk about this book, then, Prue.'

There was a loud squeal of a ringtone from my bag, one that I recognised: Erica was calling. I fumbled to get my phone out but somehow missed the call anyway – 'Bollocks.' – so I set it flat to watch for a voicemail.

'Work?' Connie asked in a smug sort of tone. I bit back on reminding her that my work paid her husband's debts.

The small chirp announced a voice message and I clicked in to listen. I held my phone to my ear and mouthed, 'Sorry' to my sister even though I wasn't. But it felt like the right thing to do, given that I'd ignored her last comment completely.

'Prudence. Sorry, Prue, it's Erica. I know we're due to see each other tomorrow but I'm afraid I'm going to have to cancel.' She paused and let out a hearty cough. 'I'm just feeling so unwell and I... I don't know that I'd manage. Don't assume a meeting. I'll call you. Take care now, won't you?'

The next voice I heard was an automated one, giving me options to save, delete, panic. After I'd saved the message, I put my phone back inside my bag but left the top of the screen sticking out enough for easy access in case she called back. I knew she wouldn't – but there was a strange sort of hope in me all the same.

'We're both just joking, Prue, about all the work stuff,' Connie leapt in when I looked back to them. 'I only know you've been swamped with it,' she said softly, then, as if she were trying to console me. 'And that your living room looks a bit like a crime scene, with all those corkboards and everything about the place. Like, oh, I can't think of the film,' she clicked her fingers in a way that made me think of Erica clicking away evidence, 'you know what I mean, though, where detectives have got all that red string tying one clue to another, pinning points on maps and that sort of thing. You know, right?'

'I know.' I tried to join in the humour. 'The corkboards are for two separate projects though,' I added. It was the first time I'd admitted it out loud.

'So, can you talk about either of them?' Connie asked, and Robert shifted forward in his seat. He rested his elbows on the table and looked at me, money-hungry, as though I were about to serve him something.

'Honestly? Not really. I'm sorry, Con.'

And I really was. But the NDA was ironclad – and in many ways, I was writing the same book twice.

# CHAPTER TWENTY-SIX

What's the word for when hunter becomes hunted?

There were only so many favours that Yusuf was willing to lend me. He might have been happy to talk through the details of Hannah. But after my second unanswered call to him – and no calls, still, from Erica – I decided his generosity must have run dry. I was going to have to find another way to track down Detective Fowler. There were so many filmed interviews with him, though, I hoped it would only be a matter of time before someone in the know let slip about where he was hiding. In the time since Roger's case, Fowler looked to have made a nuisance of himself to anyone who would listen when it came to the Millers. *So why hasn't she mentioned him?* I scrolled through another interview, this one a written transcript where he talked through the details of the case; leaning heavy on the more damning bits of evidence. On the face of things, he looked to have retired since Roger. I couldn't help but wonder, though, whether he'd left the force willingly or whether he'd been helped off the premises for disorderly behaviour.

The search results stretched back page after page. The more I read, the more irked I became. Though not at Erica or the project – only at him, for what he was saying about her. Fowler must have made it a mission to talk to as many outlets as possible but, Erica was just letting him have free shots at her without hitting back, I thought, with another stroke of the trackpad.

'Is it because you don't care, Erica, or because there's some truth here?'

Even with that thought in mind, though, I couldn't redistribute my annoyance. I wondered whether I felt closer to Erica now she'd kicked me to one side. She seemed like the sort of woman who might bring that out in people. I reached to the other side of the sofa to grab my phone, thumbed into my contacts and down to her name. It had been four days without a text or a call and I was growing suspicious of the silence. But I'd listened, relistened, to the voicemail message where she clearly said she'd call me. I hit the side button to lock the handset, sighed and threw it back to the other side of the seat. In time with it landing, though, it started to ring and I grabbed at it like a horny teenager who'd been waiting for days on a crush; which was in some ways true. When I turned the handset over, in the desperate hope of seeing Erica's name, I saw that it was a blocked number instead. *Silly girl, it wasn't even her ringtone,* I scolded myself in a voice that felt less like my own and more like hers. *And she never calls on a blocked number.* But I answered it anyway because, *what if this time she has?*

'Prudence Carr speaking.'

'I've heard you're looking for me, Miss Carr.' I recognised the voice from the documentary – and the too-many recordings I'd watched over the last two days. 'Forgive him, Yusuf knows I'm a private person but he passed on your number all the same.' He chuckled. 'Apparently he doesn't mind breaching your privacy.'

I had to laugh. 'No, no one seems to these days.'

'You're working on the Roger Miller case, then, are you?'

'More like the Erica Miller case,' I admitted. After all, if he was going to help he needed to know where my interests lay. 'I know you've spoken quite openly about the case and your time working with her. I wondered...' *Christ, what do I wonder? What do I need from you?* 'Look, might I be able to buy you a drink? Cup of tea somewhere?' I checked my watch; it was the wrong hour to go meeting a stranger. 'Tomorrow? It's meant to be a nice day, maybe we could–'

'You don't need to woo me, Miss Carr.'

'Prue. Please.'

'The same truth stands. I'll thankfully accept tea and I'll openly talk about that woman, mind you. Half eleven tomorrow suit you? I could meet you outside Bounty Park?'

'I know the place, sure. I'll wait by the entrance?'

'You can,' he laughed again, 'but you'll recognise me sooner than I will you.'

'I'll be wearing a hefty backpack and holding two cups of tea.'

'Very well. I'll look out for you.'

'Thank you, Detective Fowler, I really–'

'Just Grant will do now.'

He ended the call before I could correct myself. I wondered whether "that woman" would get the blame for his change in title when I met him.

---

Detective Fowler – Grant – looked more dishevelled in person than he had on the documentary. I wondered whether they'd brought in hair and make-up at the time, to give him the appearance of someone more reliable when it came to an expert testimony. In real life, he was wearing a floral print shirt that was too bright for the hour of the morning we were meeting, and there was a brown liquid stain that had dripped down the front of it. He wore a thin jacket, too, unzipped and flapping in the morning breeze. The sunlight looked to make him wince a little and he shaded his eyes as he made his introduction – 'Morning, Prudence.' – then he snatched away the tea I was holding with the urgency of a man in need of caffeine. *Which is exactly the sort of man you look like at the moment*, I thought as I took a measured sip from my own cup. He dug one hand into his pocket and shrugged with awkwardness, as though he'd forgotten why we were there. On the walk to meet him, I decided that I expected new truths – or accusations – to erupt from him like water from a broken fountain, spouts shooting everywhere with a mix of fresh and muddied ideas. But he looked as though he were waiting for me to take the lead now.

'Thank you for agreeing to talk to me about this,' I started.

He laughed. Air rushed out of him, and I thought I caught a waft of alcohol. 'Honestly, it's about all I'm needed for these days. Since I left the force–'

'You took early retirement, is that right?' I butted in. I made a move to start walking, then, so he didn't have to look at me while he decided whether or not to lie. I'd done my research since our call. From my peripherals I saw him rub at the back of his neck then look down at his feet rather than ahead. I wondered whether it was shame, or whether he needed to concentrate on his walking.

'They pushed me out, in truth.'

A knot unclenched in my belly; *at least you're going to be honest.*

'After the Miller case, my reputation wasn't what it used to be.'

'Because Erica Miller got away?'

He made a noise like I'd winded him. 'No. More that I couldn't accept she'd got away. Everyone on the force has a case, like, *the* case they can't shake. Throughout the investigation, she became mine. After, the folks there warned me not to make a mission out of her, told me it would be best to let it go.' He paused and sipped his tea; I left quiet between us. 'In hindsight I should have done. But there's a lot of stuff that looks different in hindsight, isn't there?'

I thought back to the day I signed the contract with Erica. 'There really is.'

'You said you're researching the case?'

'I'm interested in Erica, primarily. What evidence there was, how that held up – or didn't, so I'm led to believe.' I remember Erica's click of the fingers, then, her whoosh. 'It was only circumstantial evidence that made it through to court, wasn't it?'

There was another laugh but this one was hard-edged, angry. 'Apart from the blood.'

'Blood?' The same knot that had only just loosened began to form again.

'In the living room. We found blood that had been cleaned up when we swept the house for evidence. I told them about it, on that new documentary. But I don't know, some people say they want to know; some people want to make good television. Either way, they chose not to include it. What can you do?' He pointed to a nearby bench. 'Seat?'

'Sure.'

The pair of us were angled to look over the park. There were tulips bursting with colour and choruses of children spilling out of different corners. It felt too nice a place to be having a conversation like this one. Still, I tried to nudge Fowler along.

'Why isn't the blood better known about? I can't remember seeing it listed as–'

'It became circumstantial; part of the catch-all. She had a good explanation for it.'

Without even hearing Erica's explanation, I could already believe it would be a convincing one. 'What did she say?'

'Nosebleed. Apparently, Roger was prone to them. There's no evidence to suggest that but of course, why would there be? Handy, too, isn't it, that she picked something that would explain blood while also explaining why there weren't extra wounds on the body.'

I tried to piece together his meaning but, 'I'm sorry, I don't...'

'Let's say we find blood, evidence of a fairly substantial amount of blood, and Mrs Miller says, well, my husband fell and gashed his knee open. Then, days later, we find poor Mr Miller bobbing about on the coastline and when we look at the body, there's no gash in his knee. Like any good detective team, we'd go back to Mrs Miller and say hey–'

'Where's the gash,' I ended his sentence.

He snapped his fingers. 'Bingo. She's a smart woman.'

*But that doesn't make her a murderer.* 'Was there anything else?'

'Loads,' he said before launching into a string of evidence; all of which Erica had already told me about. I knew about the alibi, the coastal getaways, the– 'Of course there's the affair.'

'Whose affair, sorry?'

He snorted. 'Fair question, that. But Roger's. Although there were rumours, too, that old Mrs Miller was having her way with someone as well.'

I swallowed down my dislike of "old". It was just like a man to describe any woman over thirty as ageing, hoary, decrepit; *focus, though, because he might be onto something here.* 'The woman actually came forward, spoke to us directly, but when push came to shove she couldn't go through with the official testimony and,' he shrugged, 'I mean, without that, what's anything worth?'

'Did she say why?'

'She was scared, I suspect. We didn't exactly have huge amounts to go on. Motive was hard without her word on the affair and no one in the world likes a murder case on their shoulders so she just went away. I kept in touch with her for a while after the case ended, told her she'd be safe and all the rest of it. She wanted to move on though.' He sipped his drink again and I realised I'd been so rapt by his retelling that I'd forgotten to drink my own. 'You might know of the woman, actually,' he said, in a knowing kind of tone.

'Why would I know–'

'Hannah Wilcox?'

The cardboard slipped clean out of my grip and lukewarm tea landed in my lap; on the floor, on the bench, even– 'I'm so sorry, did I get you?' From instinct I brushed at Fowler's jeans until it dawned on me that I was invading the space of a stranger. 'I'm sorry, I shouldn't have... Christ, sorry.'

He laughed again. There was phlegm in the noise, and I wondered if he were a smoker. 'So, you do know her?'

I tried to brush myself clean, rub the remaining drops of tea from my spill into my clothing. 'She was having an affair with Roger when he died?'

'According to her word, yes.'

'That's all you've got to go on?'

'That's all we would have needed to create reasonable doubt. She said, she said would have been enough...'

# CHAPTER TWENTY-SEVEN

What's another word for confession?

Erica shook the packet of cigarettes, as though weighing the contents, then pulled out another. She held the box out to offer me one but I shook my head; I never smoked without a drink. Although I was dangerously close to asking for one of those. This was our first meeting in a week and Erica seemed changed from the last time I'd seen her. Everything she shared, she shared in a hurry, as though she might forget the words if she didn't part with them soon enough. We talked about Roger's affairs – 'One woman even got in touch...' – and the ramifications for their marriage – 'I don't know whether she expected to ruin a marriage...' – and Erica's bank account; or her father's, I wasn't fully certain: 'She had a price just like the rest of them.' She didn't name anyone and I didn't ask, but the question knocked against my teeth all the same. I kept my head bowed and my hand scribbling.

'People always crack for the right sum in the end, don't you think? Tea?'

'I'm sorry, wait...' I shook my head. This was the first time she'd needed my involvement in the conversation for at least half an hour. 'No, I don't– no, thank you. Erica, did you not worry that one of these women might have had something to do with Roger's death?'

'They didn't.'

I reached up to my face; brushed one cheek then the other, as though checking for bite marks from her snap. She'd made the words sound vicious – certain.

'Besides,' she carried on, faced away from me and filling the kettle, 'by the time Roger went missing it had been nearly a year since he'd had an affair.'

*Except that's not true.* I paused my scribbling. *Does she not know, or does she not want* me *to know?* 'Do you know why?'

She turned to face me. 'He and I were closer. He mightn't have felt the need anymore. We were more like friends by then, but I think that happens to all married couples with time. I didn't push him away, though, and... I didn't do much else either. You know,' she sounded jovial, 'like pay for an alibi or stage my innocence, or buy the best legal team money could afford. I didn't become estranged from my father, I didn't call on friends in high places, I didn't seduce the jury.' She reached for another cigarette, struck her lighter and inhaled hard. The burn of the paper filled the room for a second. 'It made me a sensationalist superstar in many ways, riding on the coat-tails of the women before me.' She laughed and smoke charged out of her. 'Perhaps I should scrap the memoir entirely and make a collage novel as a homage to Wilkie Collins. What do you think?'

I wasn't sure whether the question was rhetorical, so I kept quiet. Erica hadn't needed much goading to this point so I thought more would come.

'All I want is the chance to tell my story, Prue, that's all I truly, desperately want. That's all any woman ever wants, isn't it? I wanted to do it in my own time, too, but apparently that's a bit too much to ask.' She tapped her chest as she spoke; kept her hand flat there while her torso expanded with another pull of smoke. 'Although by this point in our dalliance I'm sure there are things you want to know yourself.'

Erica caught my eye then, and held my stare for an uncomfortable time. The look she gave me felt heavy, as though she were alluding to something in particular. *Does she know about the extra research?* I wondered then, but I couldn't see how. *Unless she's been doing her own...*

'There are things I need to know, for the sake of the project.'

She flicked the cigarette from the doorway then settled back into her seat again. 'So, ask.'

'Where were you the night Roger went missing?'

It wasn't what I wanted to ask, but it was the first question my reaching mind laid a hand on. Erica's head twitched, like something had flicked her ear by surprise, and then she narrowed her eyes as though inspecting the question for booby traps. I wondered, then, whether she'd been braced for me to ask worse; *the* worst question I could think of. But despite her strange demeanour and her eye for deceptive details, I still couldn't believe Erica was a murderer. She was a woman scorned, sure, but weren't we all sometimes? I thought of my own mother and the bitterness she held for Dad; the man who didn't love us enough to leave his wife, such was his moniker. But Mum wouldn't have gone after him with a heavy instrument, and I'm led to believe his wife didn't either.

'Prue?' Erica pulled me back. 'Are you asking for the book or yourself?'

I weighed up my answer. 'Both? The former is more your decision?'

She screwed her lips up at one side; I imagined her weighing the truth against a lie. 'I was with a man named Marcus. He's a prostitute although I'm led to believe sex worker is the preferred term now. He put a lot of graft into his profession, though, so he deserves a name of his own choosing. He and I had been seeing each other for two years, fairly regularly. We had sex, we talked, sometimes we sat quietly and kept each other company. I paid him a handsome sum for the times we spent together, and my father paid him a handsome sum again to keep his mouth shut.'

The shock hit me like a backhander to the face. 'Your dad knew?'

'Prue, my father knew everything. But you've seen the things printed about me in the media, without evidence for most of it. Can you imagine the scandal if they knew for certain the company I was keeping?'

I imagined they'd feel the same as I did: surprise; disappointment; outrage? *Do you feel that because she's a woman, though?* The thought filtered in after, through the cracks of feeling. But there was a weight to the idea, too. There had been more than a few media scandals about men who had been caught using sex workers, and what had been said of them? How long did we hold it against them? It occurred to me, then, the likelihood of Erica carrying this humiliation for longer than a male counterpart was motive for her to keep it quiet. *But does that mean I believe it?*

'Where is Marcus now?' I asked, my pen hovering.

'You want to check my alibi.' Although it was a heavy accusation, she threw it as though it were a featherweight one. My head snapped up at the suggestion but before I could open my mouth in protest she added, 'I never knew his surname, Prue, why would I? If you want to play detective, I remember Dad once mentioned a transaction or two being made to the University of Bournemouth. Business Management, I believe. You could trawl the admissions records for a Marcus.' She half-laughed. 'Assuming that was his real name. Everyone likes their privacy in the workplace, though, don't they?'

Her eyebrow arched. The question felt like a pointed one.

'Erica, I'm not sure I follow.'

She stood, then, and flicked the kettle to boil for a second time. But rather than finding a cup, getting a teabag, sourcing milk, she reached for the cigarette packet on the window and shook another free. She stood in the doorway to light the end and exhale the first pull into the garden. Then she threw the lighter on the work surface with a clatter.

'It's the journalist in you, isn't it? Your kind are always sniffing out a story. So,' she pulled, held it in, steamed it out, 'Roger and I argued the night he went missing. He had a retirement plan to source more property down on the coast; although what work it was he felt he was retiring from, I wasn't sure, and I said so. "This is the only enjoyment I have", he said. "*Money*", I said, "money is your only enjoyment?"' She paused for a drag of her cigarette and then stared hard somewhere behind me.

I didn't want to turn and look. I thought she must be reliving it all then. *How clear is your memory of it?*

'I told him, plainly again, if he enjoyed money so much then maybe it was about time he started to make some. I was losing money from his last botched investment series and I, *we* needed to recover from that before we threw money elsewhere. I was tired of going to Dad for help with this sort of thing. I wanted us to recover on our own.' She pulled in hard again but immediately coughed out the fumes. I'd never seen her smoke so much. 'He called me a cruel woman. Prue, can you imagine that? Cruel and controlling and... hideous things that a husband shouldn't say to his wife, especially a wife who's paid for that husband ten times over. He left and I was livid, furious, so I called Marcus. He came over to the house and we – what have you. Then he went home. When Roger still wasn't back after that, I called my father to be angry for a while longer.'

She flicked the cigarette end into the garden and crossed to the other side of the room. There was a drawer at the end of the kitchen work surface that she yanked open with a fury. She pulled out an old handset, a Nokia, and threw it from a distance to land hard and clatter on the table. 'That's the phone I called Marcus from, before calling my father later in the evening.'

*Another confession then.* I wanted to reach out and touch the phone, pocket it, like Erica maybe wouldn't notice it was missing. But I bit back on the urge. This was the most she'd given me of that evening and I couldn't risk anything that would startle her. I only listened quietly, like a woman held hostage, while Erica set about making a cup of tea through a series of angry slams.

'Over the years there were one or two others I met with.' She set two steaming drinks on the table and added, 'And that's the phone I used to arrange meetings. Unlike my husband, you see, I knew how to keep more than just myself happy. I didn't boast my affairs to people; I didn't sleep with homewreckers.' She paused, sipped her drink and swilled the tea around her mouth as though washing away ash. 'I didn't shit where I ate.'

I wrapped my hands around the mug for something to do. When nothing more came, I stole a glance at her from under hooded eyelids. Her breathing was erratic, as though she were panting, and there were small splodges of red appearing on her face and neck. She looked like she were wearing blusher two shades too dark for her cheeks, and it made the shape of her jutting bones uncomfortably clear.

'Are you okay?' I managed.

She huffed and shook her head. 'That isn't what you want to ask.'

'Erica, I don't–'

'Okay, let me ask you something?'

My stomach clenched. I didn't like where this was leading but there was no way out. I nodded. 'Okay.'

'How carefully did you read your non-disclosure agreement?'

It hadn't been what I was expecting. 'I understand that this work will be your work, of my writing but written under your guidance. I don't have a claim to the book and–'

'Ah,' she held up a finger, 'you don't have *any* claim to the book?'

I shook my head. 'That's how ghost-writing works.'

'Hm.' She smiled, not at me but more to herself, as though a plan were forming – or as though realising a plan had worked.

Balls of anxiety knocked together in my gut like a Newton's cradle.

'Now, your turn.'

It felt like I'd been taken by the hand down a path I didn't want to see the end of; not only now, but through the whole project. I somehow knew what it was that Erica needed from me but, despite her need, it pulled against my own set of wants. I didn't *want* to ask this question; I didn't *need* for this to be what happened next. So instead of asking I stated it like a certainty, 'You didn't kill your husband.' I counted out the seconds that made up the space between my saying it and her not responding and then, again, but with an intonation; I gave her what she wanted. 'And you didn't kill your husband?'

She stared into her tea for another few seconds. When she looked up, she only smiled.

# CHAPTER TWENTY-EIGHT

What's another word for dead air?

I tried to sit with music on but everything felt like static. Since leaving Erica's earlier in the day, the world had faded to white noise and I felt single-focused; a dog suddenly unleashed from its pen at the track. Cross-legged on the living-room floor, I was on my second glass of wine when I opened the manuscript that I knew I shouldn't have been writing. Erica had made it uncomfortably clear that I was hired to write a story; the story she told me. But then there was book two – the rabbit out of reach around the course – that no one had even known I was writing. I clicked between my document and Erica's, and back again. After so many switches that my screen started to lag, I opened up my non-disclosure agreement. Arthur had told me that he'd looked it over and that there wasn't anything unusual to be mindful of. But he'd missed something. We both had.

The PDF unfolded and I clicked to the search box: DEATH. The word appeared, highlighted yellow, and I dragged my cursor along the clause that neither Arthur or I had taken the time to read.

'The thing is, Prue,' Erica had explained earlier in the day, 'the non-disclosure only exists as long as I do. When I die, which will be sooner than we both imagined, in fact, that little slip of paper disappears along with me.'

'That's not how they work,' I'd pushed back, and she'd laughed. It was a harsh noise, curt and throaty; the sound of someone experienced dealing with naivete.

'That's how mine works. Ask Colin, why don't you?' She'd pulled out her phone then and searched for his number. 'It's out of hours for him really, but he'll answer if he thinks it's me. Go on,' she'd hit the green button on my behalf, 'call him, really.'

'Erica?' He'd answered on the second ring, and she'd looked so proud of being right. 'Erica, is everything okay?'

'Colin, it's Prue, sorry, it's not... Erica is here, she's fine.'

There was long pause. 'She's told you.' Colin's voice was heavy with disappointment and I wondered what conversations they must have had about this already.

'About the clause? About... about the end of the NDA.' I hadn't known how else to phrase it. 'She's told me.'

'You'll be free to write whatever you want after Erica has died, Prudence, you understand of course. But whatever she wants you to write at the moment is what you're bound, by contract, to set down. There's no wiggle room on either of those truths.'

'I don't– Colin, I'm sorry, but I don't understand. What am I meant to be–'

'Write what she tells you to write, Prudence. It's as simple as that.'

Erica must have heard him, too, because she huffed a laugh, raised an eyebrow. 'See.'

'Thank you, Colin. I'm sorry to have bothered you.' Even though *I* hadn't. I disconnected the call and handed the phone back to Erica. 'You think I'll kiss and tell; write a second book from this?'

She slid the phone back to her side of the table. 'I think you're already writing one.'

---

I had managed 500 fresh words on Erica's manuscript when I emptied my third glass of wine. I hit save, then locked my screen and moved to the kitchen. My stomach grumbled with the acidity of alcohol against its lining, but I wasn't sure I could manage solid foods. Instead, I poured another generous measure into the glass; kept pouring until the bottle was near empty. There was a small amount left still, hardly worth leaving it behind. Instead, I upended the bottle and drained the last of it straight into my mouth. I banged the base of the empty on the work surface with a force that showed my inebriation.

'Bollocks.'

My mobile hummed alive from the living room but I didn't rush to answer it. It would be Max or Luke or– someone else who needed for me to be normal. After that afternoon with Erica, I wasn't sure I could manage the charade for long periods of time. I was slow-moving from one space to another, feeling along the walls of my home that no longer felt like a safe zone, so much as it felt like a cave of secrets. I imagined mildew and confessions and–

The phone rang again. It was Erica's tone. And this time I did rush.

'Hello.' The vowels were longer than they should have been. But at least I'd made it to the sofa without causing myself any harm.

'You sound drunk.'

'Oh, that'll be because I am.' I'd never taken such a tone with her. But already I knew Future Prue would apologise profusely, blame the alcohol and the trash-can fires of panic that were clouding Past Prue's brain. 'It's out of hours.'

'But you answered all the same,' she said, and I thought she sounded smug. 'I needed to know that you're okay.' She paused, but I sensed there was more coming. 'And to remind you that you're bound by contract, and that you told me earlier that you–'

'Would be fit and well for an extra day's writing tomorrow,' I finished.

'Is that still the case?'

I didn't know whether she were referring to a specific part. Still, I said, 'Yes, Erica,' as though answering a schoolmistress; my signed agreement a catch-all to anything she expected.

'You won't be okay to drive.'

'I'll just be a touch later than usual but I'll be–'

'I'll send Colin to collect you.'

'No, Erica, really–'

'Sleep it off, Prue.'

She disconnected the call.

I slid from my sofa down to ground level and sat in front of the laptop again. The non-disclosure was the first document to come to life when I hit the trackpad, but I quickly closed it. Instead, I hit the keyboard function to pull up the remaining two documents side by side: the books. I scanned the opening of one, compared to the most recent paragraph I'd written for the other; their ends and beginnings to date were a stark contrast.

One, I knew, would build on the lies; add to the canon of what she didn't.

But the other would tell them all exactly what she did.

III

---

# AFTER

# THE THINGS I DIDN'T DO:
## A MEMOIR BY ERICA MILLER

There are times in life when our silence serves us. We make an armour of it, to protect ourselves and those close. Then, there are times when our silence condemns us. In my life, the muzzle I placed around my own tight jaws has achieved both these things.

Now, though, I think less of my life and more of my death, fast-approaching. We all exist in this hourglass; sand running through our fingers, filling our shoes. My hourglass has turned to lie drunken, heavy and lopsided. With that turn my desire to remain mute has also shifted.

I, Erica Miller, of sound mind, have so much to say that I wonder whether this book will burst free from its spine; I imagine pages unfit for the density of words. People may come to this expecting a deathbed confession. I have wondered who the reader might be, whether they will arrive thirsty for traces of iron between the floorboards. If that is the case, Imagined Reader, then you'll be disappointed. The only iron between the floorboards of my home came from unexpected menstruation; bloody noses; failed concentrations when playing at being a chef. There will be a falsified alibi though. There will be truths and confessions like those never reported before because that was and remains my intention in writing this book. It isn't a manual of murder nor a rehash of police statements. There are quite enough books claiming to be the former and already far too many leaks of the latter.

Instead, these will be the details missed during the reports on my husband's death. These will be claims that were never shared with the media, names that should have been shared with the police, and a confession that has remained the same since I first told detectives, No, I did not do it.

I still did not do it. And in these pages, Imagined Reader, you will find the final truth of the matter: the many things I didn't do.

---

There wasn't much for me to collect from the office. Arthur had always asked freelancers not to leave too much of themselves behind week by week. Still, there was a tall locker that I had filled with copious amounts of crap in my years. I took my time in emptying it, like it was something to be savoured. The reluctance that weighed around me felt like a shawl; knitted and itchy uncomfortable. It had to be done, though, because someone else would take this locker soon enough, now I was vacating the premises, and I didn't want the corner of half-chewed gum to be the legacy I left behind. Since Erica I'd managed to cause quite enough trouble, left behind enough office chatter, without also being The Dirty One who didn't clean out her mess. I half-laughed; *no, you revel in your messes instead.*

I checked my watch. It wasn't long before I had to leave the building for the last time. My new apartment was a closer walk than my old one had been, at least, so I could take home the pack of stuff I hadn't been able to part with and throw it into the box room for a Future Prue to deal with. I thought of my office mementos sitting there alongside Roger and Hannah's wedding album and smiled. After everything, I'd managed to make contact with Hannah to ask whether she wanted the scrapbook or not.

'Christ, I never even thought of what had happened to that,' she'd said, breathless. I wondered whether my phone call had winded her. 'What will happen to it if I don't have it?'

I'd sucked in a greedy lungful of air to rush through my answer. 'Erica told me to take whatever I wanted or needed, as long as no one else laid claim to it. Now, I'm only too happy for you to have it. I can arrange for it to be couriered to you, wherever you are, or... I don't know, a drop-off point somewhere if–'

'Thank you, Prue, but if you can find use for it then I think you should have it.'

'You don't want those memories?'

There was a smile in her answer. 'I think I have quite enough of those.'

Hannah had told me to keep in touch but I wasn't sure whether she'd meant it, so I hadn't. I'd left my number with her, though, to signal the door was wide open for a day when she might want to talk. She was bound to have questions.

*Everyone will...*

I stacked notebook after notebook from base to brim of the box I'd brought with me, and then wedged in memories around its edge. The chewing gum I carved out of the corner crease of metal with a butter knife and then I dropped both in the bin with a fondness that felt disproportionate for the action. But maybe it was just the satisfaction of seeing something clean.

Arthur had asked that I step into his office before leaving. So I heaved the box up, half-closed the locker and left the padlock for it on the sideboard in the staff room. The vultures would fight over it when I was out of the way. In the end, to save further spats, I imagined the locker being used to store stationery that nobody needed. I didn't mind the idea of that being the thing that filled my space.

When I was three steps from the open doorway I heard Arthur on the phone inside, so I hovered. I wasn't trying to listen in. But at close range to a conversation, it's impossible not to hear when you're being mentioned by name.

'Prue will clear out today.' He sounded sad about it. There was a long pause, then, and I wondered who he was talking to. 'She's cleaning out the corner locker at the moment. Christ knows what's in there... No, she won't budge, I've tried... She's compromised now, she won't... Why would she be a ghost-writer now she's got a book waiting under her own name?' Another long pause, longer than any of the others, and I craned my head that little bit closer to the door. 'I know some writers do it, but she won't... Because this is what she's always wanted.'

I said exactly the same thing to my reflection every morning: 'This is what you've always wanted.' When I saw slurs on social media or advertisement campaigns for the book; good or bad, I thought, *Remember, this is* exactly *what you wanted.*

The phone landed with a thud that brought me back into the buzz of the hallway.

'Anybody home?' I knocked on the door as I entered. I was leaving, I reasoned, so I had long ago done away with the need for office niceties.

'Usually when people knock, they wait.' Arthur smiled.

I looked around the room, then, and asked, 'Oh, were you busy?'

He narrowed his eyes. 'You were listening.'

'I wouldn't.'

'You did.'

We remained in a stare-off; Arthur's seasoned glare bearing down hard on my own.

'Okay, I did. Who were you talking to?'

'A colleague,' he answered too quickly. 'He heads up another firm and he was telling me what a fool I would be to let you go.' He raised his eyebrow as he spoke, as though he weren't entirely convinced of the truth behind the comments. 'I've been thinking that already for years, though, and the sudden skyrocket to stardom makes no difference to me. Seat?'

I rested on the visitor chair. 'Stardom seems a stretch.'

'How's the six-figure book deal treating you?'

I shrugged. 'Fair point, assuming I've got a story that will sell.' My working relationship with Erica was out in the open now, but the fruits of that remained to be seen.

'You're all ready to go, I see,' he nodded to the box then looked back at me, 'I hope you cleared out the gum from the corner.' He held a hand up, to pause my response. 'Don't tell me, either way. I want to be surprised.'

Arthur and I had relaxed into an easier relationship since I'd told him I was leaving the agency. It was a thought that hadn't crossed my mind at all until he mentioned it – 'You'll be leaving for a life of writing under your own name, I suspect?' – and then, as though I'd given it hours upon hours of consideration, I answered, 'Christ, I suppose I will.' He'd asked that I work long enough to finish my outstanding projects – books and articles that felt only too easy to write in the shadow of Erica – and I said it was a fair notice period. He'd given me a bonus all the same, too, as though I'd been significantly inconvenienced for finishing a job I'd long loved doing. I would miss the bustle, the interviews, the one-to-one sessions with clients; my stomach turned and I saw a flash of Erica's face then, that I had to blink away.

'Prue?'

'Sorry.' I shook my head. 'Gum?'

'We'd moved on from gum. We were onto your final payslip.' He was leaning over the table with an envelope in hand. 'You'll also find all the boring paperwork in there that you'll need assuming you ever get another job.'

I snorted. 'Because I'm such a pain in the arse to work with?'

'You quite know that that's not what I mean.'

There was a long spell of dead air between us. I hadn't been prone to sentimentality before Erica; since her, even less so. Still, Arthur had welcomed me with open arms some years ago and he'd unleashed me with the same kindness. Something in me wanted a better gesture than a hurried thank you.

'Arthur, would you like to come for dinner at my home?' The question came out in a rush with one word knocking into another. But at least I hadn't backed out. 'You're welcome to bring a wife,' I took a quick glance at his hand; no ring, 'or partner, kids even. But not kids that are small-small because I don't know what to do with them, and there are a lot of sharp edges around the place.'

He spluttered a laugh. 'I'm too old to have small-small kids at home. But dinner would be lovely, Pruden– Prue.' He rolled his eyes. 'I'm sorry, I don't know why I still call you that. Did you have a day or time, or... Maybe we can decide another time?'

'You'll keep in touch?' I asked, in the same way I'd asked Hannah. People had trod with caution for the last six months or more, and I was wary of forcing my company on anyone. The door was open, though, the oven preheating; the sofa desperate for someone on the other side. 'I'll be working from home even more so now, so whenever, I'll be around.'

'Okay, well, I'll go ahead and call you.' I smiled at his

promise then, and moved to stand up. 'You're heading out, got everything sorted and ready?'

'Yes and yes. I've got an appointment across town in an hour or so and I want to dump this at home first.' I picked the box up and balanced it against my hip. 'As soon as I move to one side of the city, all my meetings are moved to the other.'

'First world problems, kid.' He laughed. 'Meeting with the dreaded editor?'

'Worse,' I answered, 'lawyer.'

# THE THINGS I DIDN'T DO:
## A MEMOIR BY ERICA MILLER

Death is made up of nuggets; immeasurable weights. I have carried the burden of Roger's death, and I will carry it further. This mess of murder took my father, too, who I firmly believe would have had some years ahead of him, had he not been buying silence and staging alibis for me. The two men in my life were men who, largely, took care of me. Although they occasionally set me aside to take care of each other. But perhaps they can't be blamed for the allegiance of their manhood. Given their propensity for caring for me, it only seems right that this book is dedicated to them; particularly as without my husband it wouldn't exist, and without my father instilling in me a fierce burst of adrenaline from a young age, I wouldn't have had the courage to write it.

Imagined Reader, there is a real possibility you will find fault in these pages. It may be you have seen or heard or read something to the contrary of my accounts. There have been times when even I've read something written with such conviction that I've felt inclined to believe something that I knew all the same to be untrue. Lies are designed to deceive us in that way. In research and discussion and further writing, though, we can lift the veil that others would have us hidden behind. That, I hope, is what this book has done.

There was nothing overtly dramatic in Roger's death, for me. He left after an argument about money; something many married couples argue over. He stayed out for an evening; something many husbands and wives will have done. He stayed out longer still; something he'd been known to do before.

When the police were called, I was compliant with their investigations and despite hours of questioning I complied, still, with what they needed from me, all the while mourning my husband. All the while, little did I know then, that my father was nursing cancer that would eventually swipe him from me, too.

When they arrested me, I did everything required to make the process a smooth one. When they released me, I was led to believe that was the end. It was only the beginning for so many things, though, including this book.

To be plain in my final dedication then: I thank my father for guts and grit enough to fight any situation. And I thank my husband for having died – although it wasn't by my hand.

---

Colin's office was exactly the look of old-school legal firm that I'd expected it to be. Since Erica, we'd met perhaps a handful of times but never on his own turf before now. It unsettled me. But at least I knew he couldn't make a scene with his colleagues sitting only a wall-bang or a loud shout away.

When she died, he held me accountable for her behaviour in the last months of her life. I had started to refuse meetings with Erica by then, although I was still in constant contact with her. I would send over pages and she would hurriedly send back edits, many of which didn't make sense. Although by that time in our artistic coupling, I had decided to bow to Erica's needs and wants. I'd given in on the point of a confession already; arguing over a semi-colon seemed petty and unwise, given what I knew of her. When the manuscript was finished – edited to within an inch of its life, and my own – she stopped replying to my messages. I only received one from Colin then – "Consider this a termination of your contractual obligations to one Erica Miller." – to formally excuse me from any more involvement with the script. He hand-delivered the letter, too. I realised soon after his arrival, though, that he had done so in order to corner me in the hallway of my old apartment building, envelope in hand as though wielding a deadly weapon.

'What did she tell you?' he'd said, with the urgency and discomfort of someone who knew precisely what it was that Erica had to tell. I hadn't answered his anger, though, and only told him to ask Erica; I had even suggested that he read the book.

'I'm sorry, he's running a little late.' The secretary pulled me back into the present and flashed me a smile that made me think she wasn't sorry at all.

'That's fine, thanks.'

The room was all swagged and tailed, complete with leather armchairs, too. It could have been stripped from a piece of cinema playing homage to a gentleman's club from the fifties. With that in mind, it came as no surprise at all when I skimmed the certificates pinned to the wall in their dark wood frames; boasting one male name after another. There was a small printout, too, listing the first-aid officers, HR liaison; and so on. But I noticed there was nothing about an equality and diversity policy. *They probably imagine that as woman's work*, I thought, before shaking my head and checking the time again. He was running nearly twenty minutes late now. I wondered whether he was, though, or whether he was lingering on the other side of the door. It was easy to remake Colin into a cartoon villain. Was he twirling a moustache, smoking a cigar; only waiting for me to burst in with my best Hey-Look-Here-Mis–

'Prudence.' His voice caught me off guard. 'Do you want to come in?'

I was long past correcting his use of my full name so I only stood, smiled and followed instruction. I imagined that was what the women in these parts were expected to do. Although there was little rationale, then, to how he'd managed to work with a woman like Erica for quite as long as he did.

Colin trod round to the opposite side of the desk, leaving me to take the visitor's chair. The décor of the room matched that of the main office outside; there was nothing here to make someone feel comfortable: *Which is probably how he likes his clients.*

'How are you keeping?' he asked, his face already buried in paperwork.

'I'm doing well, thank you, Colin, and yours–'

'Well, also.' His head snapped up. 'I know my instructions on inviting you here were a little vague. So I'm glad you've made the time to come down. I'm not interfering with the workday?' I only shook my head; it felt like a fishing query and I didn't want Colin to have more information than he needed. 'Very well. Look, I won't string this out for longer than necessary but there are some things that have to be cleared up about Erica's estate. You understand, I'm sure. She had no living relatives so the majority of what she owned has gone to charity. But there is this.' He leaned forward to slide a slip of paper across the desk to me. 'I realise the amount may have changed but she said this should cover things, to the best of her knowledge.'

I reached for the paper. 'I'm not sure that I–'

'Please just check the amount, if you would, Prudence, and

I'll need you to sign here.' He followed this with a larger slip of paper and a fountain pen that I thought would likely have cost more than my monthly wages would allow. 'It's only to confirm you've received the cheque.'

I took the pen without looking at him; I couldn't take my eyes off the written figure. It more than cleared my debt. So she had been watching, I knew then.

'Prudence, can you sign?'

'I'm sorry, of course.' I followed instructions and left a shocked version of my signature on the page before sliding the sheet back to him. 'This was really generous of her.'

'Yes,' he sounded unimpressed, 'no matter how people treated her, Erica always did have quite a forgiving nature.'

The comment was a pointed one; sharpened and dipped in poison. So I ignored it and only folded my cheque in half, before stashing it in the back pocket of my jeans. If the rest of the meeting could yield only pleasant surprises, then I thought we may both make it out unscathed. The wing-flutter of hope in my chest soon settled on a precarious branch, though, as Colin struggled to get a much larger envelope free from a nearby drawer. There was nothing written on the package from what I could see. It was only the thick brown parcel paper, designed for bulk items, but with no address to guide it. Colin glanced across to me, as though checking that I were watching, before dropping the package from an unnecessary height, so that it landed on the desk with a thud loud enough to cause a knock on the office door.

'Everything is fine, Ava,' Colin shouted without breaking his stare on me.

'For me?' I asked and he nodded.

'The manuscript.'

I reached over and set a hand flat on the paper. Like touch memory, I saw a montage of hours spent with Erica; there was laughter sandwiched around tension. Whenever I thought of her, the memory of finding out what happened to Roger was never far behind. I shuddered at the thought now. But I didn't have to try hard to remember the smash of rain against my windscreen and the fourteen missed calls on my phone from Erica by the time I'd driven back into the city. The voicemail – 'You were hired to complete this job, Prue, and that's exactly what I'll be expecting you to do.' – and the creeping realisation that she was right.

'There are further details contained herein,' he rested another envelope on top of the one containing the book, 'relating to publication of the work.'

'I'm sorry, I don't know that I plan to publish it, Colin, in truth I–'

'It may be out of your hands,' he interrupted me, then leaned back in his chair with a cocked eyebrow that made him look the part of a schoolmaster; me, the part of an unruly child. 'When you finished the manuscript, Erica started to submit the work to publishers and agents as far as Scotland and London. There may even have been one or two international names mentioned toward the end, you'll have to check. That second envelope, on top, is a list of those who she submitted the work to, and the dates that it was sent. Many of them have turnaround times of months and months on end, of course, so she knows...' He winced at his phrasing. 'She knew she was unlikely to see the fruits of her labour in print, but she thought, perhaps, you may stand to gain something from the work being published.'

I couldn't hurry the information through. 'I think I need a minute, I'm sorry.'

Colin's expression was blank. 'Of course. If you have any questions, you're always welcome to call reception and they'll put you through if I'm available.'

*And if you're not?* I thought. But I didn't overlook the

implication that it was time to go now; that I could let this weight sink in somewhere other than Colin's prized visitor's chair. I reached forward to collect the manuscript and paperwork from the desk, and for a moment wondered whether I'd tumble back down under the weight of them both. But Colin raised an eyebrow, flashed a thin-lipped smile, and held out a hand without standing.

*Take the man's hand,* I told myself, *and have your breakdown elsewhere.*

# THE THINGS I DIDN'T DO:
## BY P. CARR

### Foreword – draft

I had/have always wanted to write. From a young age, I would write stories that bored my family members to tears. I would encourage word-play games with friends [Scrabble? Are there any others worth mentioning? Ask Connie]. I would voluntarily write the essays of classmates; if it involved reading a book beforehand, even better. When I wrote my way through to university [named?] I decided journalism would be where I was best placed. The bustle of a hectic city with papers, print and deadlines to keep me fuelled looked to be a dream; worsened by the films I watched as a teenager, too, wherein the writer often doubled as a superhero or a super-sleuth. If I could grow into someone who existed between Superman and Jessica Fletcher, I would feel like I had arrived [are these references too dated?].

Ghost-writing had never entered this plan. But journalism didn't quite live up to the lifestyle I'd planned for either. There wasn't work wherever I turned; the city didn't need another naïve hopeful with a voice recorder and a bright smile ready to take names and tell a story. There were some people in the city, though, people with good money in their pockets, who were in desperate need of a writer. That's how I found Arthur; the chief of the agency I worked for [should the name be listed here?]. I worked there for some years, on a range of fun and exciting projects. Then, towards the end of my career as a ghost-writer, a new type of project came in; a long-form memoir, wrapped up tight in NDA-print paper with a gleaming gold ribbon on top. Like the hungry writer I was, I tore into the packaging, signed to say I'd received it and then–

I met Erica Miller.

Things to include still:

General outline of an NDA for people who don't know – should probably inc. this earlier than this break point.

Should I give an outline of the plot here or does that give too much of the story?

Check with Dylan how much info to include.

Ask Dylan about names – should/can I be naming people or do I need their permission for that?

---

I was stumped for words. I'd walked the length of my office so many times that Apple Health notified me I was beating my daily average. When the hum of my mobile cut through the quiet of the apartment, I leapt on the handset like a puppy might leap on a treat.

'Hello?'

'Were you sitting on it?' Dylan joked. Her tone was jovial, familiar. I'd come to know her sounds well. 'I'm only calling to check in and see how the final chapter is coming along. Is there anything you need for the draft, anything I can be doing?' She paused for an intake of breath but then jumped back into speaking, 'Do you have wine?'

I laughed. 'I have two bottles. One for while I'm writing and–'

'Another for when you've finished?'

'I might be being optimistic in thinking I'll get through both tonight.'

'It's best to be prepared, though, Prue. You're doing the right thing.'

If anyone overheard us, they would guess at a more serious conversation topic than how many bottles of wine were stocked in my fridge. But Dylan knew how much of my writing process hinged on the familiarity of things being just so. Max and Rita had joked that I was as tortured as the rest of them, now I'd made it. Meanwhile I was still shifting around uncomfortably against the idea of having made anything. Still, it seemed fair that when writing something that made me so hideously uncomfortable, I could at least surround myself with small creature comforts of home. I sipped my wine and exhaled hard.

'How's everything with Erica's manuscript?' I asked then.

'Is that what's bothering you?'

'It isn't bothering me,' I lied, 'but I know it's near completion. An update can't hurt.'

'We're looking at a September launch. The cover hasn't been approved just yet but we're working on the final options for that. You'll have a say, though, so don't worry. I know we agreed on that.' In the months that I'd been working with Dylan, she'd always kept to her word. Still, my nerves wouldn't settle. 'Is there anything specific you wanted to know about, or just a general update? I want to help however.' She spoke softly, then, as though talking to a gremlin that might startle easily, which I suppose is what I am now.

'How are the reviewers reacting to it?'

'Prue, honestly, that's the least of your worries at the mo–'

'Can you just…' I petered out as a dull pain thumped my temple.

'It's blowing up. Early reviewers are staggered, and people are asking after the sequel.'

The sequel being my book; the book I was meant to be writing the final chapter of.

After Colin gave me the manuscript, I waited for the surges of interest in Erica's story. I was so stunned by his Evil Genius reveal that waiting felt like the only thing I was capable of. The responses were mixed to begin with, with some publishers asking for the entire manuscript and others asking whether it was a hoax. For those who wanted the whole book, I wrote back accordingly to explain the script had changed ownership; did it matter? It mostly didn't, as long as I could prove the legalities of it all. After, there were one or two who found themselves drawn in even further by the twists of Erica's story, which was of course *my* story in disguise. During this fishing expedition, Dylan was one of the editors I reeled in. She worked at CLF Publishing, a firm that specialised in true crime, crime and thriller. She pitched my idea to her team, and they offered a two-book contract within a week.

'There isn't a second book though,' I'd said, starstruck by the offer.

Dylan smiled. 'There will be if you write one.'

I had recordings enough, research enough to support my claims against Erica; enough, at least, for CLF not to worry about my writing in more detail about her – about my time with her. 'Besides,' Dylan had asked, 'who is there to dispute what you're saying about the book?' She was right, too.

So, within a month of meeting Dylan, my shiny and excited new editor, I signed the contract for *The Things I Didn't Do*; a book that CLF bought worldwide rights to, complete with the option for an audiobook if they could find the right narrator.

'Unless you want to record the book yourself?' Dylan had suggested; I sensed she was testing the waters but at the time I couldn't proffer a reply. It was all too much too soon. Erica's book would be edited, tweaked and tightened and, far from being Erica's book by the end of the process, it would be my first authorial claim, followed by the sequel–

'There's no rush for you to get this finished right now, you know that?'

There was though. Even though working with Dylan had been a fun and informative experience in equal measure, the closer I got to a completed draft of my own work, the greater my desperation to be done with the project. I knew that Erica's manuscript was already a hornet's nest of conspiracy theorists and deniers, just waiting. What would those same people do when my own story arrived?

'It would feel good to get it off my plate, I think.' I clicked between my document and Erica's on my laptop screen. Then, for another strange creature comfort, I opened the non-disclosure agreement. 'Did you look at the draft of the foreword I sent over?'

'It's next on my to-do list.'

'And you'll–'

'Send edits as soon as I'm done.' Her words were cracked with a smile. There was a long pause, then, while I flitted between documents and Dylan, in the style of someone contending with writers all day long, looked for the best way to approach me. 'Prue, why don't we grab some dinner tonight, what do you think?'

*The softly-softly approach.* I smiled. She must think I'm close to burning out. 'Tomorrow?'

'Tonight.'

There was another long pause while I scrolled to the bottom of my manuscript. *One more chapter...* 'Tomorrow. You can buy me steak to celebrate.'

She laughed. 'Expenses can run to that. Can I call later, to check in?'

'If my phone is off then I'm writing, so don't panic?'

She murmured in agreement. It had only happened once before, when Dylan had worried to such an extreme that she'd wound up on my doorstep, out of breath and banging for me to open up. She'd found me, headphones on and half-soaked from a bubble bath. I hadn't let her live it down yet.

'Don't work yourself to death, though, Prue, okay?'

'Because I'm a wealthy asset or because you care?' I joked.

'Will you hang up if I just say yes?' She matched my tone. 'I'll call later. Answer.'

'I'll try.'

Before she could protest any further I disconnected the call and set my phone to airplane mode. I poured another splash of wine into my glass, paced the room another three times, and then pulled out the emergency cigarettes from the top drawer of my desk. It was my fourth smoke that day, even though I usually limited myself to one; first thing in the morning with my coffee. But stressful times called for more regular vices.

# THE THINGS SHE DID
## BY P. CARR

From a young age, I have always wanted to write. I carved a life for myself from this desire to pen words and share them with a rapt reader; someone who might carry my phrases with them for the rest of the day, share them with a friend or leave them idly on their coffee table at home for a guest to pick up. For some, writing is a job. For me, it has always felt something more like a vocation. What would you do if you could do any job in the world, friends used to say, and I would look at my desk and my paper strewn about and my post-its with reminders only decipherable to me and I would say plainly, 'This. If I can do anything, I want to be doing just this.'

Erica Miller didn't choose me because I'd always wanted to be a writer. But we worked so well together for that reason. Erica fed me story after story and I documented it all as well as I possibly could. Better still, alongside that, I knew I was writing something people would want to read. Whether they knew they were my words, or whether they truly believed that the words had been stripped from the tongue of an accused murderer.

The word *accused,* though, is where I should pause.

Erica and I were working late one evening when she told me what had really happened to her husband, Roger Miller, on the night he went missing.

Prior to this she had confessed to her father falsifying an alibi for her for that same evening, as well as explaining to me in detail how her father had also provided financial bribes to anyone who may have been able to contradict his alibi for Erica. Erica's father, while being a reputable businessman in many respects, looks to have spent much of his life laying a paper trail of pound notes over the mistakes that his daughter made.

Her marriage to Roger turned out to be one such mistake; his murder, a bigger mistake still. But Erica admitted freely that her father would always protect her, so, on the night Roger died, she called on her father for help again.

During an argument about money, Erica hit Roger over the head with a glass-and-silver trophy; one gifted to the couple at a charity gala some three weeks before, for their work in supporting the organisation. Erica did not plan to kill Roger; nor did she realise entirely what she had done until she watched his breathing slow, and the blood come. So she, like any one of us may have done, called her parent for help.

The rest of that story I will set down in the pages that follow, to explain how Erica Miller got away with murder.

For many, I understand this will read as a work of contradiction. There are some parts of the story that will stay the same from Erica's own work and some that will change; there are some elements of Erica's work, though, that were never true to begin with, and I will address those here as well. In working with Erica, I was commissioned to write a manuscript; that is precisely what I did. I followed instructions and set down Erica's narrative of life with and around Roger. It took me some time, though, to understand what Erica was truly asking of me with this project, and indeed what she was gifting me: two manuscripts. The first book to be published by CLF, *The Things I Didn't Do,* co-authored by Erica and myself; and this book, *The Things She Did.* Across the two scripts the truth of Roger Miller's murder will take different forms; that is, Erica's word against my own.

Which of course, now, it always will be.


# THE END

ACKNOWLEDGEMENTS

Through every book, I have a group of friends who steadfastly support me and listen to the woes of writing: Beth; Daria; Dan B; Ade. The Bloodhound Books author group, too, is another space where I can – and often do – turn for a good rant about this writing life. These people are never shy with their advice and they never fail to pull me through any sticky moments in my plots – of which there are many, with the narrators I use.

For this particular book, though, another note of thanks needs to be afforded to the University of Wolverhampton. While writing, I was also teaching on the Popular Culture MA where week after week the students and I would discuss representations of a notorious serial killer (Jack the Ripper, no less) in different media forms. We considered graphic novels, films, television series and, of course, sometimes newspapers. How these killers are adopted by different areas of media productions became fascinating to me; though it feels a tad morbid to admit sometimes. I spent a lot of time thinking about the female killers in this scenario, and how they had and hadn't been kept in mind by the media, in the same way as some male counterparts. There's a more complicated conversation waiting to be had there, I'm sure. But these thoughts wouldn't have had the space or time to root and flourish, in the form of this novel, if it weren't for the teaching hours and the student engagement on the Pop Culture course. To those students – should you ever read this – a hearty thank you, and the same thanks to my colleagues for gifting me the opportunity to talk about hardened criminals for a couple of hours each week. I don't mind admitting it was a joy – and Erica and Prue wouldn't be quite the same without that experience.

Finally, Reader, whoever you are, thank you for sticking with my unreliable women. There are more coming...

# A NOTE FROM THE PUBLISHER

**Thank you for reading this book**. If you enjoyed it please do consider leaving a review on Amazon to help others find it too.

**We hate typos.** All of our books have been rigorously edited and proofread, but sometimes mistakes do slip through. If you have spotted a typo, please do let us know and we can get it amended within hours.

**info@bloodhoundbooks.com**

www.ingramcontent.com/pod-product-compliance
Lightning Source LLC
Chambersburg PA
CBHW020801190726
48285CB00006B/2126